"W... I just wanted to make sure you didn't think I was trying to...rekindle something, that's all."

The thought of rekindling anything with Colleen filled Aiden with a raging heat he did his best to ignore. "Hey, I'm on the same page. The last thing I want is to relive our history."

She scowled, creating cute creases between her eyebrows. "Why don't you tell me how you really feel?"

He stared at her. "I'm sorry if that sounded cold, but both of us know that we need to keep our distance."

Colleen nodded, wishing he didn't look so yummy in his khakis and polo shirt that displayed his well-muscled arms so wonderfully. His masculine scent teased her.

Oh, how she wanted to snuggle close to him and have him wrap his strong, capable arms—

She cut that rogue thought off, reminding herself that she wasn't here to wish herself back into Aiden's life....

Dear Reader,

I've put together a list of Silhouette Romance New Year's resolutions to help you get off to a great start in 2004!

- Play along with our favorite boss's daughter's mischievous, matchmaking high jinks. In *Rules of Engagement* (#1702) by Carla Cassidy, Emily Winters—aka the love goddess—is hoping to unite a brooding exec and feisty businesswoman. This is the fifth title in Silhouette Romance's exclusive, six-book MARRYING THE BOSS'S DAUGHTER series.

- Enjoy every delightful word of *The Bachelor Boss* (#1703) by the always-popular Julianna Morris. In this modern romantic fairy tale, a prim plain Jane melts the heart of a sexy playboy.

- Join the fun when a cowboy's life is turned inside out by a softhearted beauty and the tiny charge he finds on his doorstep. *Baby, Oh Baby!* (#1704) is the first title in Teresa Southwick's enchanting new three-book miniseries IF WISHES WERE… Stay tuned next month for the next title in this series that features three friends who have their dreams come true in unexpected ways.

- Be sure not to miss *The Baby Chronicles* (#1705) by Lissa Manley. This heartwarming reunion romance is sure to put a satisfied smile on your face.

Have a great New Year!

Mavis C. Allen
Associate Senior Editor

Please address questions and book requests to:
Silhouette Reader Service
U.S.: 3010 Walden Ave., P.O. Box 1325, Buffalo, NY 14269
Canadian: P.O. Box 609, Fort Erie, Ont. L2A 5X3

The Baby Chronicles

LISSA MANLEY

SILHOUETTE *Romance* ®

Published by Silhouette Books

America's Publisher of Contemporary Romance

This book is dedicated to my very own babies,
Laura and Sean, who have grown up letting Mom write.
Thanks for taking care of yourselves and for being so
enthusiastic about my writing career. You two are
the best kids a mom could ever ask for.

 SILHOUETTE BOOKS

ISBN 0-373-19705-5

THE BABY CHRONICLES

Copyright © 2004 by Melissa Manley

Visit Silhouette at www.eHarlequin.com

Printed in U.S.A.

Books by Lissa Manley

LISSA MANLEY

has been an avid reader of romance since her teens and firmly believes that writing romances with happy endings is her dream job. She lives in the beautiful Pacific Northwest with her college-sweetheart husband of nineteen years, Kevin, two children, Laura and Sean, and two feisty toy poodles named Lexi and Angel, who run the household and get away with it. She has a degree in business from the University of Oregon, having discovered the joys of writing well after her college years. In her spare time, she enjoys reading, crafting, attending her children's sporting events and relaxing at the family vacation home in the Oregon coast.

Lissa loves to hear from her readers. She can be reached at P.O. Box 91336, Portland, OR 97291-0336, or at http://lissamanley.com.

MEMO

To: Colleen Stewart, Staff Reporter
From: The Boss
Subject: THE BABY CHRONICLES

Colleen—*The Beacon* will be running a feature entitled THE BABY CHRONICLES. This new story will include pictures of cute babies coupled with your copy.

I'm assigning you to this story.

To give the feature a unique edge, I'll be bringing in a freelance photographer. You'll meet him as soon as he's back in town, and you'll find out about the exciting plans he has for this article. [Be nice to him…or else.]

Congratulations on your new assignment.

Chapter One

Colleen Stewart shifted uneasily on the hard chair across from her editor's large, metal desk, holding back a ragged sigh.

Cold, hard dread inched through her. She had to find a way to get out of writing this article. She would never, ever be able to write "The Baby Chronicles" without letting all of those smiling, cooing, bald little toothless angels turn her heart to mush.

Mush she didn't need.

"I don't see what the problem is," Joe said, yanking his stained yellow-and-red tie loose. "All you have to do is write about cute babies. Piece of cake."

Cute babies a piece of cake? Hardly. "Joe, I turned down this assignment a week ago," she said, deliberately excluding the reason she'd talked her way out of the job in the first place. Joe would laugh his head off. "Nothing has changed. I still don't want to do it. Can't you get someone else?"

He waved a hand in the air. "No can do. Rudy left town for a family emergency and Christy has her hands full covering the budget cuts at the school district. You're it."

Colleen bit her lip. "What about Angela?"

"On maternity leave."

"Steve?"

"I fired him this morning."

She flinched but kept at it, leaning forward. "Zack?"

"You're *it,* Colleen." He pulled his bushy, gray eyebrows together and scowled. "What's the big deal, anyway? Just supervise the shoot and write the story, all right?"

She'd love to tell Joe why this seemingly harmless assignment was a big deal for her. But she couldn't. Joe was a hard-line journalist and a traditional family man from way back. He would never understand her need to stay away from things like endearing babies, cute little animals, large, close-knit families and nice, lovable men. She'd learned long ago that there was no sense in hanging around things she could never have.

Things that made her ache inside.

She opened her mouth to refuse, but Joe's ice-hard glare stopped her and she clamped her lips closed. Further argument was useless. She prided herself on her ability to get through tough situations with strength and self-control, just as she'd made it through her neglected childhood all by herself. She'd write this article while remaining unengaged and unfazed by the undoubtedly adorable babies. She had to. Her job as a reporter at the *Beacon* and her protected little world here in Portland, Oregon, depended on it.

"Anything else?" she asked, trying to sound upbeat. She glanced out the window, hoping the blue-skied, puffy-clouded summer day would cheer her up.

"Yeah, actually there is one more thing. We're bringing in a freelance photographer for this spread."

A psychological cloud moved across the sun. Her gut tightened. Ever since she'd been shuffled through the foster-care system, meeting knew people always made her feel off balance and vulnerable. "Really? Why?"

Joe shrugged. "The guy's good, and he offered his talent for dirt cheap. Wants to build a career photographing kids. Thought this would be a good opportunity." He looked over her head and smiled. "Ah. Here he is now."

A barely perceptible, woodsy scent drifted across the air, teasing Colleen's nose. She froze, momentarily confused, and a long, heart-pounding second later, recognition thudded into place. Only one person she'd ever known had smelled like a combination of trees and wind and the great outdoors.

Aiden.

But that was impossible. Aiden was overseas in some godforsaken, war-torn country taking pictures.

"Taking pictures," she mouthed.

No. No way. She was imagining that outdoorsy,

distinctive, heart-stopping scent, right? Aiden Forbes was thousands of miles away right now. He was absolutely, positively not standing behind her, ready to take over his new, unlikely job as *baby* photographer.

Almost incapable of movement, she somehow pressed a shaking hand to her fluttering stomach. A chill rushed up her spine, scattering goose bumps over her entire body.

Please don't let it be him, please don't let it be him. She'd broken up with Aiden eight years ago because he'd shown her, by loving her so completely, how incapable of loving *she* was.

Aiden was just a painful reminder of the unfixable flaw inside her and of all of the ramifications that flaw had had in her life. With Aiden around, she'd never been able to forget the defect that had made her parents ditch her into the foster-care system.

A deep, hauntingly familiar voice scraped across her raw nerves like a rusty chainsaw on metal, dashing her stupid hopes. "You must be Joe Capriati." From the corner of her eye she saw a large, tanned hand reach to Joe over her shoulder. "I'm Aiden Forbes."

Time slowed to a crawl. In the millisecond it took Colleen to draw a choked, desperate breath, her world tilted on its axis and almost sputtered to a stop.

She pressed her other quivering hand to the side of her face and bent her head, ridiculously trying to hide, even though she was dying to look at Aiden and see how the years had changed him. But she didn't look, she couldn't even move. Maybe he wouldn't recognize her.

Of course he would. He wasn't popping his head in for just a moment. He was the photographer on the story she'd just been assigned. She was going to have to work with him. Side by side. Photographing precious babies.

She closed her eyes and shook her head, wishing the floor would open up and swallow her whole.

Aiden Forbes, the only man who had ever been able to crack open the door to her flawed, vulnerable heart, was back.

Shaking Joe's beefy hand, Aiden's attention remained stuck on the seated woman he'd had to reach over, her blond, curly hair spilling down her back like wavy, near-white gold. She had a hand pressed to the side of her face, trying to…hide?

Something in the set of her shoulders seemed familiar, but he couldn't put his finger on why. He'd only been back from Bosnia for a week, and he certainly hadn't met anyone with that kind of hair.

Only one woman he'd ever known had had hair like that…

Nah. Couldn't be her. Colleen had always said she'd blow this town as soon as she could. She was long gone by now, out of his life forever.

His curiosity and male awareness got the best of him, though. Would this woman have a face to match those long, perfect curls? As he pulled his hand away from Joe, he leaned sideways to get a look at her.

His heart stalled.

It *was* Colleen.

A jolt of stunned surprise exploded in him like a Scud missile going to ground, and the day she'd busted his heart into a million pieces flashed in his brain. Surprisingly sharp pain knifed him, as if she'd walked out on him yesterday instead of eight years ago.

I don't love you, Aiden. I never will.

Her parting words still ripped through him like a tropical typhoon, jabbing at the rough scar she'd carved in his heart.

He mentally recoiled from that burning ache, hating the bitter reminder of the love she hadn't returned, of how she'd walked away, leaving his dreams of a home and family in the dust.

The hellish years he'd spent photographing things most people saw only in their nightmares had honed his recovery skills to a fine point. But recovering from the shock of unexpectedly seeing the only woman he'd ever loved sitting right here, bringing all of the old pain and gagging bitterness to the surface, was damn hard.

She dropped her hand and looked the way he felt when he'd blown a whole roll of film. Tiny lines had formed between her delicate eyebrows and her plump, perfectly made-up mouth—painted in the same pink, totally hot shade she'd always worn—was pressed into a tight line.

"Colleen Stewart," he drawled, hoping to keep the

clawing pain inside him from showing. "That glad to see me?"

She slanted a gaze up at him and smiled a fake little familiar smile, the one she used when she didn't want to talk, the one he'd seen often and always dreaded. Her intense blue eyes, which reminded him of the sky on a perfect summer day, sparked. "You have no idea."

He lifted an eyebrow and tightened his jaw. What the hell was her problem? She'd dumped him on his butt, not the other way around.

Even though they'd only dated for two months, he'd been ready to sacrifice his dreams of being an international photojournalist to settle down and marry her, wanting the kind of traditional family he'd grown up in. But she'd blithely shredded his heart. In pain, he'd dived headfirst into another life, which had only led to more pain.

Images of suffering children exploded in his brain. Doggedly, Aiden held the horrific memories at bay, not wanting to go down that familiar, ache-filled road right now. But he would eventually. Oh, yeah, he would. For years while overseas, and even now, his nights had been reserved for that particular torture.

Eventually, his sleepless nights spent in the throes of nightmares had caught up with him and he'd begun to make tactical mistakes, putting his own life at risk. His best friend had given it to him straight—it was time to head home to a job that wasn't going to cost him, or someone else, their life. Aiden had agreed, unable to function, and came home to something more life-affirming, something meant to eradicate the memories of the babies he couldn't save.

Joe cleared his throat, dragging Aiden away from his awful memories. Joe looked back and forth between Aiden and Colleen. "You know each other?" He plopped his rotund body back down into his creaky leather chair.

"Oh, yeah," Colleen muttered, pressing her mouth into a tight smile. "We go way back. Don't we, Aiden?"

Even though he was bugged by her flip tone, he managed to smile at Joe, not wanting to come off as difficult. He needed this job. Badly. "Colleen and I went to journalism school together." *And I was stupid enough to fall in love with her.*

"Ah. Well, good," Joe said, inclining his head. "Saves the getting-to-know process." He looked at Colleen. "Colleen, since you're familiar with how we put these articles together, why don't you take Aiden to your office and fill him in." He looked back to Aiden. "And you fill her in on the plans we discussed on the phone."

Aiden's stomach plummeted. He jumped his gaze to Joe. "She's the reporter?"

Joe nodded. "Yup. Is that a problem? She did a great job on 'The Bridal Chronicles.'"

Damn. Colleen was the last person Aiden wanted to work with, the last person he'd ever wanted to see again. The bone-deep bitterness he'd felt when she'd thrown his proposal back into his face and ended their relationship reared up like a cobra and bit him hard.

There was no way he was going to stir up and relive all kinds of bad feelings—pain, betrayal, bitterness—by working with her.

Slow down, Forbes. This job was his best shot in Portland to gain some attention as a baby photographer. No, he wasn't about to make waves and come across as difficult to Joe and he wasn't about to let Colleen take control of his life again. He would find a way to work with her, even if it killed him.

Aiden arranged his mouth into a smile. "No, not at all."

Joe smiled. "Good. Hey, one more thing. I have to tell you, the photos of the kids you sent in with your portfolio blew me away. Got any more?"

Aiden suppressed a shudder at the mention of the graphic black-and-white pictures of children he'd taken, unable to stop remembering their haunting poignancy. He'd only brought them out to snag this job and never intended to look at or deal with them again. "I gave them to my mom," he said truthfully. "I have no idea what she's done with them." He hoped his tone conveyed how final that explanation was. Nothing could convince him to haul out those photos again.

Joe nodded. "Ah. All right."

Aiden looked at Colleen, needing to move on to getting started. "You ready?"

Colleen widened her blue eyes, apparently surprised that he was agreeing to work with her. Hell, *he* was surprised he was agreeing. But this job would be worth it.

After a long pause, she tersely nodded and stood, smoothing her skirt. Aiden couldn't help giving her a quick once-over. He had to admit she'd matured well. Her once slender college-girl's body had blossomed into a curvy, womanly shape, displayed perfectly by the figure-hugging, knee-length navy blue skirt and jacket she wore.

He stepped back and gestured for her to pass him. "Ladies first."

She scooted past, her eyes averted.

Her scent washed over him—fresh, tangy peaches—stirring up his senses as it always had. His male radar kicked into high gear and he watched her walk away, appreciating her long, willowy legs and the way her rounded hips moved beneath her tight skirt.

His blood began to percolate. Great. The absolute last thing he wanted was to get a renewed case of the hots for Colleen. Bad, bad idea.

But, boy, did she look good…

What the hell am I thinking?

He'd returned to Portland to reestablish ties with his large family and to get rid of the guilt and dark memories his time overseas had embedded in his brain. He hadn't come back to get tangled up in a mess like Colleen. She might call to him on a male level he didn't have much control over, but there was no damn way he was ever going to let her get close enough to knife him in the heart again.

Feeling marginally better, he said goodbye to Joe

and left his office. Nope, Colleen didn't have the power to affect him any longer.

After the anguish and searing heartache she'd put him through, he'd make sure of it.

"I can't let him get to me," Colleen said to herself, a bad habit she'd picked up during her early childhood, before foster care, when her parents were always gone and she hadn't had anyone else to talk to.

She repeated the words over and over again as she hightailed it toward her office, desperately hoping that if she said the words she would magically be successful.

But she was a realist. She'd quit believing in magic when she was six and her mother had chosen to spend Christmas with her boyfriend in a hotel room, and her father had taken his new wife on a cruise rather than spend the day with Colleen. She'd been left alone for the day and most of the night, huddled on the couch, watching Christmas movies, tears streaming down her cheeks. She'd been forever changed on that cold, gray day.

Her innocent love and faith in her parents, along with her little girl's belief in magic, had died a quick, inevitable death, only to die all over again when they abandoned her to the foster-care system when she was nine. One thought had cemented itself in her brain then, and had a profound influence on the rest of her life. There was something missing inside her, some flaw that kept her from being able to love and nurture a relationship, even with the two people who were supposed to love her no matter what—her mom and dad.

No, there was no use hoping for a magical solution. She was going to have to deal with Aiden—which meant getting rid of him. He was going to step into her office and she would be sucked back into his appeal. Oh, how she remembered his heart-stopping green eyes, keen sense of humor and wide, generous smile.

And how cherished she'd felt when she was wrapped in his arms.

She jerked her thoughts away from useless memories. Feeling warm, she pulled off her jacket and flung it on a pile of overfilled file folders in the corner, then gave in to her wobbly knees and sat down behind her paper-strewn desk.

Aware that he would arrive any second, she pressed a shaking hand to her chest to calm her jumpy heart, took a deep, cleansing breath and closed her eyes for a moment, summoning up her trustworthy control. She could get through this if she remained calm, cool and unaffected.

She sat up straight a mere second before Aiden stepped into her cube, instantly filling the drab, messy little space with his large, vibrant self. She forced herself to look directly at him instead of fooling with the voluminous stacks of papers on her desk as she was inclined to do.

He simply stood in the doorway with his hands in his pockets. His shadowed eyes reflected a shrewd perceptiveness that sent a weird, hot, shivery chill down her spine.

Of course, he looked too darn good. He always had. It wasn't surprising that he was still absolutely gorgeous, the epitome, in fact, of her concept of the ideal male. Physically, at least. There was no such thing as an emotionally ideal male for someone like her.

His tall, once-rangy body had filled out very, very nicely since the last time she'd seen him. His shoulders seemed broader, his arms thicker. An impossibly wide chest, perfectly displayed by the short-sleeved, forest-green knit shirt he wore, looked firmer and more muscled, and tapered down into a taut waist and legs that were long and solid-looking beneath his khaki trousers.

His mahogany-shaded hair was shorter than she remembered, and he'd gelled the longer hair on top into a funky, spiky texture that somehow complemented his chiseled, masculine features and lightly tanned face.

But it was his sea-green eyes that, true to her memories, got to her the most. He looked at her, pinning her in place, and she was unable to move a muscle or form a coherent thought. Yes, those incredible eyes had always been able to see into her soul.

Why can't you love me, Colly?

His old question echoed in her head, reminding her of the wall he'd tried to tear down inside her, the love he'd seemed determined to wring from her barren heart.

The love she didn't know how to return.

Her shaky control almost splintered, but she gathered her composure around her like an old lady's tattered shawl, determined to act normal and calm around him even if she dropped dead from the effort, which at the moment seemed highly likely. She folded her damp hands on the top of her desk, noticing how hollow his cheeks seemed.

He spoke first. "So I guess you're not too happy to see me," he said, his voice harsh and low.

She frowned, surprised by his cold tone. Mercy, was he still mad about their breakup? "Are you still upset about…what happened?"

He pressed his mouth into a harsh line. "Of course not."

She wasn't going to argue with him, but his tone and expression suggested he wasn't being truthful. Even so, it wouldn't hurt to apologize. She'd always felt guilty for breaking up with him, even though it was the only option open to her. "Good. But for the record, I'm sorry for what I did…walking out on you."

He snorted. "Yeah, right."

She pulled in her chin. "You don't think I'm sorry?" Figured. They had never been on the same wavelength emotionally.

"What I think about what happened eight years ago doesn't matter." He pierced her with those intense, emerald eyes. "You just look damn unhappy to see me."

He always was too perceptive. "Why would you say that?" she asked, cursing the hitch in her voice.

"Oh, come on." He stepped closer. "You look like you have a stick up your…uh, well, you just look pretty unhappy."

"I'm not particularly happy or unhappy to see you," she said, lying. At this moment, she would have been happier to see Jack the Ripper, who would spare her and just kill her. But Aiden, well, Aiden had the ability to make her bleed inside, just as her parents had, and that terrified her.

He snorted under his breath and rolled his eyes. "Still the same old Colleen."

She bristled, but then reminded herself whom she was dealing with here. This was *Aiden,* for goodness' sake. He'd always had the amazing, frightening ability to turn her inside out. She would go to her grave before she'd let that happen again.

A slow, hot burn started in her chest. Thankfully, anger was the one emotion she could handle right now. Embracing her anger, she deliberately stood, placing her hands on her desk. She stared him down. "How dare you sashay in here after eight years and take up where you left off, badgering me. You don't have a clue about me."

He didn't flinch from her caustic tone. Instead, he looked at her for a long, significant moment, and then leaned in so that only inches separated their faces. His pine-clean scent hit her like a Mack truck and his nearness sent hot tingles of awareness shooting through her body. And darn if her hair didn't almost catch fire.

He drilled her with sharp, assessing eyes. "I know

you well enough to tell when you're royally pissed off. You never were very good at hiding *that,* were you?''

Her cheeks warmed even more and she jerked away, needing to breathe in air that wasn't tainted by the big man in front of her. She took a deep, shaky breath and fought the urge to check her hair.

Mercy, she didn't want to deal with Aiden and his unwanted emotional analysis, she never had. The day he'd asked her to marry him and she'd had to walk away, her flaw oozing like acid inside her, she'd realized that she was so emotionally incomplete she'd never have a normal life with a family of her own and a man who loved her.

Over the years, she'd learned to deal with that harsh reality, but here Aiden was, picking her apart, dredging up memories that were best forgotten, pain that she didn't want to go through again.

She tore her gaze from his and sat down, swallowing a huge, burning lump that had grown in her throat. ''Look, none of this is relevant,'' she said, her voice quivering. ''Let's just talk about 'The Baby Chronicles,' okay?'' She tried to smile to cover up the turmoil inside her, but all that she could manage was a half grin that made her eyes twitch.

He searched her face, then his expression softened ever so slightly. ''Hey, I didn't mean to upset you.'' He rubbed his neck and cast a quick glance at the ceiling. ''I was just a little ticked off that you couldn't even manage to give me a cordial greeting.''

Now she felt like a total louse. She *had* given him

a pretty shabby reception. She met his gaze and gave him a genuine smile. "I'm glad you're okay," she said, unwilling to say she was glad to *see* him when she really wasn't. "You just…threw me off guard. I was upset about having to take on this assignment, and your showing up when you did was just a bit too much to deal with all at once."

"Hey, I'm not that happy about the situation, either." He frowned and his mouth thinned. "Are you upset about having to take this assignment because you have to work with me?"

Of course. "I didn't know I'd be working with you until you walked in," she said, uncomfortable with sharing the truth about needing to put a wall between herself and things like cute babies and…him.

"Then what's the problem? From what I've been told, the last two features, on—what were they—?" He dropped into the rickety metal and plastic chair jammed in the corner of her cube. "Brides and bachelors?"

She nodded.

"Apparently those features were hugely popular and increased readership for the *Beacon*. I would think you'd want the byline."

"Yeah, well, you'd be wrong," she muttered, gathering up the usual assortment of paper clips and pens that lay scattered across her desk.

As she sorted the paper clips and shoved the pens into her desk drawer he said nothing, just sat and stared, and she could almost hear the gears turning inside his head while he tried to figure her out.

Boy, did she wish she'd kept her mouth shut about not wanting this assignment. Aiden would undoubtedly pick her motivation apart the way he always had, in hopes of making everything "all better." And that was impossible. She couldn't be fixed—her flaw ran too deep and too wide—and she couldn't bear the sadness that would overcome her when she was reminded of that over and over again.

And was reminded of how she'd had to walk away from someone as special as Aiden.

He leaned forward, his eyes reflecting a resigned unhappiness that tugged on her heart in a way that always filled her with a dull sense of despair.

He broke the nerve-racking silence and said, "Look, Colleen, obviously you're upset about something, but I'm not going to waste my time trying to get you to tell me about it." He shook his head. "I know from experience that that would be a waste of time. So we'll skip the small talk and get down to business. All I want is to take pictures of babies. Okay?"

No, it wasn't okay. Being near him again, the possibility that he might be able to get under her skin again, absolutely terrified her. "Why do you want this job in the first place?" she asked, hoping to come up with something to get out of working with him.

He sat back, his eyes suddenly shuttered, and crossed his arms over his broad chest. "I'm a photographer. I want to take pictures of babies."

"And?"

"And what?" He looked away. When he looked

back, a dark shadow lingered in the depths of his green eyes. "That's it."

He was holding something back. What? She ruthlessly squelched her burgeoning curiosity, determined to stay uninterested, and leaped to the heart of the matter. "I was hoping you'd reconsider taking the job."

He pulled a face. "Are you crazy? This assignment could launch a new career for me. Why would I turn it down?"

Again, she wondered why he needed a new career, why he was back. Rather than give in to her nosiness and ask him, she gave him a sweet, hopeful smile in an effort to charm him into doing what she wanted. "Because I asked you to?"

"And why should that matter?"

She held up a hand and wiggled her fingers in a mock wave. "Because we're old friends?"

He laughed humorlessly, snagging her gaze again with his intense green eyes. A hot arrow of fire shot through her, relighting a compelling need, reminding her of how hot and heavy their physical relationship had been, how much time they'd spent in his bed. But sex hadn't been enough for him, even though that had been, ultimately, all she'd been able to give.

"Let me get this straight," he said, interrupting her thoughts. "You can't give me a 'Hi, how ya doin'?,' and obviously don't give a rip about our past... relationship. But I'm supposed to turn down this job because we're *old friends?*"

Shame marched through her stomach like angry

ants. She *had* been rude to him, even though she prided herself on never letting things bother her, something she'd perfected at an early age out of sheer necessity. It was time to act like the woman she wanted to be. Calm. Rational. Unflappable. She owed Aiden another apology, and she owed him this job.

Okay, she didn't exactly *owe* him the job, but she couldn't make him give up something that obviously meant so much to him, although she wondered why it meant so much to him. Did he need the money? What was going on in his life now?

Hold it. She wouldn't go there, she wouldn't let Aiden's current situation matter. She didn't care, couldn't care about him again in any way, no matter how small. She had to protect herself.

And there was one tiny little detail she couldn't ignore: he could take the job if he wanted, whether she liked it or not. And after the way she'd behaved today, there was no way he was going to be doing her any favors.

So, it looked as if she was stuck with him as her photographer. And she accepted that. She'd learned long ago, at her neglectful parents' knees, not to rail against cruel fate for very long—it never made any difference.

She threw him a sheepish, contrite smile. "You're right. It was unreasonable of me to ask you to turn this job down. I'm sorry. Obviously I overreacted." Aiden had always had that effect on her.

He relaxed back into the too-small chair and nodded. "Let's just move on, all right?"

She nodded slowly, wondering why he was letting this go, why he wasn't pressing her as he'd always done before. She gave a mental shrug, determined not to wonder about Aiden anymore. She needed to concentrate on dealing with "The Baby Chronicles." The best thing for her would be to schedule the shoot, get it over with in a single afternoon, spending as little time with Aiden and the babies as possible.

"All right," she said in a curt, businesslike voice, forging ahead. "Let's discuss which afternoon next week we'll take the pictures." She shoved a thick stack of papers aside, looking for her day planner.

"Afternoon? What're you talking about? We're going on location."

Her hands froze on her planner, still half buried beneath several old issues of the *Beacon*. She narrowed her eyes and looked at Aiden, praying that she'd suddenly become hard-of-hearing. "Excuse me?" she asked, barely moving her lips.

He leaned forward, his eyebrows raised high. "Which part don't you understand? Joe gave me permission to go on location to Sun Mountain for a long weekend. I want to take pictures of the babies outside with Mount Bachelor in the background."

· Her stomach clenched. "No way," she intoned, shaking her head. She absolutely, positively did not want to go anywhere with Aiden. Being around him had always threatened her vow to stay unengaged, to keep her heart safe. She knew from past experience that Aiden was as far from safe as she could get.

He unfolded his big body and stood, towering over

her. She slowly looked up at him and fought to keep
her jaw from falling at his imposing, utterly masculine
presence. Her heart expanded in her chest, bringing
forth the absurd desire to stand up and walk over and
bury herself in his warm, comforting embrace, to soak
up all the love he'd been so willing to shower on her.

The love she'd had to walk away from.

Sadness weighing her down, she saw the new lines
in the skin around his eyes, the shadows under his
eyes and the slight hollows in his cheeks she'd noticed earlier. His face reflected a hardness she'd never
seen before, a weariness that seemed to go bone deep,
as if he'd gone through hell. What had happened during his years overseas to cause those changes?

She shook off her curiosity, determined not to get
caught up in Aiden again. Nothing had changed; she
still wouldn't know how to love him. Not that he'd
ever want her again.

He leaned down and placed his hands on her desk.
"Yup, pack your bags, sweetheart. We're going on a
trip together." His eyes glinted with cold, hard determination. "Soon."

She sagged back in her chair and an absurd kind
of panic rose in her, almost choking her. She'd spent
years recovering after walking away from a wonderful
man like Aiden. She was finally in a place where she
was fairly happy, a place where she'd accepted that
she was destined to be alone.

Now she felt as if she was in a frightening time
warp, starring Aiden. In the last fifteen minutes, he'd
marched back into her life and turned her stable, care-

fully crafted world upside down and made her feel things she didn't want to deal with.

To make matters worse, he hadn't just stepped back into her existence for an afternoon. Oh, no. She had to go away with him for a whole darn weekend.

Damn fate, anyway.

Chapter Two

Aiden tried not to stare at Colleen's pink, open mouth, tried not to let her wide-eyed, horrified expression cut too deep. Obviously she thought going away with him was akin to taking a vacation with Charles Manson. Searching for levity to break the thick tension that had sprung up between them and calm the dull pain knifing in his gut, he said, "A fly will get in if you leave your mouth hanging open like that."

She clamped her mouth closed and glowered, drawing her perfectly arched, dark blond eyebrows together, presumably to look stern. "Very funny." Obviously she didn't appreciate his attempt at humor.

"Hey, whatever works," he said with forced lightness, determined not to dwell on the fact that he had to work with the woman who'd crept under his skin eight years ago and dismantled his heart like a one-woman wrecking crew.

"You think this is amusing?" She began to quickly shuffle through the masses of papers covering every square inch of her desk, nervously jumping from pile to pile. Odd, she'd never been the twitchy sort before.

He let out a heavy breath. "No, not amusing. But not the end of the world, either. C'mon, Colleen, lighten up." If he could deal with this after she'd cut a hole in his heart she damn well could, too.

She yanked out a sheaf of papers and began to thumb through the stack. "I wish that were possible."

"Why isn't it?"

Her worry-studded gaze flicked up and held on him for a long moment, then darted back down to peruse the papers in her hands. "I told you. I don't want this assignment."

"Why not?" he asked before he could call the words back, irritated that he cared about her reactions at all. Nothing but trouble there.

"I just don't." She shot to her feet, turned away and opened a file cabinet, ignoring him again.

He stood in silence, staring at her narrow back and blond, curly hair. A memory of her on the beach, smiling at him, the blue sky behind her, her hair blowing in the ocean breeze, popped into his brain—

He stopped the image in its tracks. Those were the memories of Colleen that had tortured him while he huddled against bombed-out buildings in the dark during cold, endless nights. Funny how those memories had also kept him warm deep inside, encouraging him to go on when scenes of death and starving children and leveled villages had cut across his heart and soul and branded themselves in his brain forever.

Fortunately he didn't need memories of Colleen to get him through anymore, to keep him warm. His new, life-affirming job taking pictures of babies would do that.

Dragging his gaze away, he fisted his hands at his sides. He had to concentrate on his work, not how his memories of her had helped him through the darkest hours of his life.

Despite that one and only benefit of his past relationship with her, he couldn't ever let himself forget that she'd coldheartedly eviscerated him. End of story. He refused to let himself care about her beyond working on this article together.

"Dammit, Colleen." He reached out and tugged on her elbow. Her soft, peachy scent assaulted his senses. "We have to work together."

She spun around and the papers in her hands fluttered to the floor. She jerked away. "Do you mind?"

He dropped his hand. She was right. He shouldn't be touching her. "All I want to do is talk—"

"We'll talk about the story, nothing more."

"Hey. Cool. That's exactly what I was going to say. So you're going to find a way to work with me so we can collaborate on a quality piece?"

She froze, staring, and a whisper of naked vulnerability flashed in her eyes. She looked down and slowly turned back to the file cabinet, shutting him out again.

He opened and closed his fists, determined not to let himself wonder or care about her vulnerability— or anything else about her. "I'm not going to let you ruin the spread. This is too important to me to let you do that."

She twisted back around and met his gaze, then opened her mouth to speak, but clamped it tightly shut. She closed her eyes briefly, and when she opened them, a studied blankness assailed him.

To his irritation, right on cue, as if he'd been plunked down in the past, his chest pulled tight. He ignored the tugging sensation, determined not to give a rip about Colleen again. He'd seen that expression before, more times than he could count. Thankfully her utter blankness, so familiar, so damn steadfast, didn't matter anymore.

He wouldn't let it.

"I...uh, I need to get something. I'll be right back." She walked from behind her desk and left him standing alone in her cube.

He swore under his breath, looked at the ceiling and rubbed the back of his neck. Casting a glance around her tiny cubicle, he again noticed the mounds of paper covering every inch of her desk and most of the floor. A yellowing, half-dead plant swimming in water sat in one corner, and its brown, dried-up twin sat on the corner of her desk. Stacks of file folders and empty office-supply boxes crowded the top of the file cabinets. The place was an absolute mess.

He frowned. He remembered Colleen as being pretty neat and well organized, and her appearance today was polished and put-together. Why was her office so filled with clutter? Was she just too busy to straighten up once in a while? And why was she so damn fidgety?

He shook his head. He had to admit, she seemed different. The glimpse of vulnerability he'd seen in her eyes earlier was totally unexpected and so unlike what he remembered about the confident, wisecracking Colleen he'd fallen in love with.

And why was she so bothered to be working with him? She'd seemed to escape absolutely unscathed by their breakup. He'd seen her in a bar the night before he'd left for Afghanistan, happily dancing up a storm with every guy in the place. Stuff like this didn't usually bother her.

Yeah, Colleen had changed. Despite that observation, she was as much a mystery as she'd always been, a mystery he would solve only for the sake of "The Baby Chronicles" and his career as a baby photographer.

As much as he hated it, to build the new life he wanted, he had to discover a way to work with her effectively.

Taking a deep, shaky breath, Colleen dropped into a chair in the small room that served as the break/lunch area for the employees of the *Beacon,* thankful lunchtime was over. She needed a few minutes alone to get a hold of herself.

To find a way to keep Aiden from getting to her.

She plopped her chin in her upturned palm and

looked around the room. The light blue walls were adorned with gold-framed copies of old issues of the *Beacon*. One wall held a new white refrigerator, shiny black dishwasher, gleaming chrome sink, speckled blue counters and white wood cabinets. Newspapers and magazines covered the surfaces of the three small, round metal tables, and unwashed coffee cups sat on the counter between the sink and microwave oven, along with an assortment of plates, empty junk-food containers and pop cans. The place was a disaster.

Kind of like her. Looked good on the outside, a mess on the inside. Mercy, she was such a product of her loveless childhood, spent first with her neglectful, flaky parents, and later, in a verbally abusive foster-care home. She shuddered, remembering the terrible, lonely place where her only purpose had been to act as a live-in baby-sitter for the rest of the younger kids and as a verbal punching bag for her alcoholic foster mother.

She shook her head, recoiling from those terrible memories, focusing on the here and now, which, un-fortunately, was inevitably intertwined with her past.

Was that why Aiden had thrown her into such a tizzy? She frowned and pinched the bridge of her nose, taking control of her spiraling, disconcerting emotions. Tizzies, she'd discovered at an early age, were useless and only brought on someone else's an-ger, targeted at her. She always made sure that she managed herself well enough to avoid them. But not today.

She'd run from her office like a frightened little girl, letting Aiden take control of her emotions.

What was wrong with her?

She didn't have the answer to that important question, just as she hadn't had the answer eight years ago. Aiden's ability to open the door to her wants and desires and her inability to fight that power had scared her to death and forced her to break up with him.

But that was then, and this was now, and Aiden was back in her life for the next few days. She had to find a way to keep an even keel, to keep herself under protective control.

A startling thought occurred to her. Had he deliberately sought her out?

No, he'd been genuinely surprised when he'd discovered he was going to be working with her. It was just an odd coincidence they'd been thrown together again. Though not all that odd when she thought about it. She and Aiden were both journalists. Also, most of Aiden's huge family probably still lived close by in Oak Valley; it made sense he'd return to Portland to be near his four siblings and parents. Just another reason she'd run, having been unable to deal with the prospect of being around his big, traditional family, light-years from her horribly dysfunctional one.

And whether she liked the current situation or not, she had a job to do. She was going to have to go away with him to complete the article. It was time to buck up and do her job without letting Aiden bother her.

Standing, she paced around the small room, forcing herself to fall back on the things that had helped her survive her childhood. Be analytical and rational. Review the situation and formulate a plan.

One. Aiden was in as photographer. Bad news, but unavoidable.

Two. They were going to go to Sun Mountain, a resort in central Oregon about four hours from Portland, for a long weekend. Again, too bad, but a done deal.

Three. Four babies and their parents, all strangers, would be going along, but she and Aiden would be the only other adults there. They would be spending long hours together, working on the article. Just the two of them, for an entire weekend…

That would be torture.

Nervous dread twisted her stomach into a knot. How could she do her job but spend as little time with Aiden as possible?

She stopped pacing and gazed into space for a long moment, her brain humming.

An idea materialized in her head. She smiled. Yes. She needed a friend to accompany her who would act as a safeguard between her and Aiden, someone she could hang out with to avoid having to deal with Mr. Gorgeous Green Eyes.

And her neighbor Maggie was just the person she needed. She was a single mom with a baby the right age. Colleen would have to pull some strings to get Maggie's daughter, Laura, included in the spread, but that was a manageable detail. She was sure she could persuade Joe to include Laura, and knew she could talk Maggie into agreeing, even though Colleen deliberately hadn't spent much time with Maggie since Laura had been born. Being around Laura, who drew Colleen's attention like a fly to sugar, was just too hard to take. And while she would have to spend more time with little Laura this weekend, which would be a test in itself, it would be worth it to have Maggie act as a buffer.

Feeling better, she clenched her hand into a fist and pumped it in the air. "Yes!" she mock whispered. Score one for ingenuity.

A male voice startled her. "Wow. You must be feeling better."

She twisted around, widening her eyes, and met Aiden's vibrant, emerald-tinged gaze. His large body filled the small room and it was suddenly difficult to drag air in.

She swallowed and pressed a hand to her chest to calm her racing heart and wobbly nerves, then forced herself to smile broadly and spread her arms wide. "I guess I am."

He hoisted a lone eyebrow. "What gives?"

A valid question given the hasty exit from her cube. "I've been thinking, and I've decided to bring a friend and her baby along on the shoot."

"Because?"

I need protection from you. "Well…because the baby is adorable, and I'd like to include her in the spread."

He moved closer, shaking his head. "I've already

approved the four kids I need for the shoot. Five won't work.''

''What do you mean you've approved them?'' She cocked her head to the side and narrowed her eyes. ''*I* haven't even seen the pictures submitted yet.''

He stepped closer still, bringing his unique clean-air and fresh-water scent with him. ''Joe e-mailed them to me this morning, and I chose the four babies I wanted.''

Annoyance rolled through her. Struggling to maintain her equilibrium, she backed up out of his scent's reach and hit the counter with her back. Aiden had had final say-so on the babies. Apparently he'd been put in charge of the content of the layout. ''Well, if you're in charge, choose one more,'' she blithely demanded, trying not to breathe in his smell, scrambling for her much-needed control.

''Can't.'' He checked his watch. ''I've designed a layout around four babies. Five will mess it up.''

Okay, Aiden was in the driver's seat, and after she'd treated him so badly today, there was no way he was going to help her out. He'd probably drive her right off the road.

Quelling the tide of hot frustration burning a hole in her chest—she hated standing meekly by, letting him call the shots—she sidestepped away from him, trailing her hand along the messy counter for support, needing space to think clearly. Chewing on her lip, she stalled, scrambling to come up with a way to get what she wanted.

"Of course," he said, his voice as smooth as silk, "we could cut a deal."

She snapped her eyebrows together and slowly turned to look at him. "What kind of deal?"

He very casually lifted a broad shoulder. "I give you what you want and you give me what I want." He smiled, flashing even, white teeth, but the smile didn't reach his eyes. "Simple."

"Simple, my foot." He was coldheartedly manipulating her. "What do you want?" she asked, even though she already had a pretty good idea.

"Your promise that you'll find a way to work with me." He stalked closer, pinning her in place with his piercing eyes. He placed his large hand so close to hers on the counter his pinkie touched her finger. "Think you could manage to do that, Colly?"

His slight touch sent sparks shooting up her arm and his use of his old nickname for her almost buckled her knees. No one else had ever called her that. Her parents, who she hadn't seen in years, had barely been able to remember her real name.

Not that he meant anything by it. He was simply trying to throw her off balance to get what he wanted, darn him. "Hauling out the heavy artillery, huh?" She smiled tightly, moving her hand away from his.

"Whatever it takes to make sure you and I can do this together to produce a fantastic piece." He looked away, but not before she saw a flash of pain in his eyes. "All I care about is taking pictures of babies."

Shoving aside her interest in the glimmer of pain

she'd seen in his eyes, she asked, "You sure it isn't more than that?"

He gave her a slight frown. "What do you mean?"

"You've always liked to pick me apart. Maybe this is nothing more than your morbid curiosity at work." He'd always wanted more than she could give, wanted to "fix" things so everything would turn out the way he wanted. But that task had been futile. She'd known from the get-go that she'd never be the traditional fall-in-love-and-get-married-and-have-babies woman he'd wanted eight years ago.

Knowing that, she should have walked away the moment they'd met instead of letting their chemistry keep them together long enough for him to care. To make matters worse, she'd had panic attacks the moment the M-word had come up, not to mention how far and fast she'd run when he'd actually proposed.

He let out a heavy breath and held up a rigid hand. "No way. I have no reason to be curious about you. And for the record, I never tried to pick you apart." He looked away, then looked back, his eyes now hard and unyielding. "Back then, I was a fool and wanted your love."

Her love. The nonexistent fantasy item he'd always wanted, the one thing her flaw had made sure she couldn't provide. "You can't have what doesn't exist," she whispered.

She sank into a chair, stunned to discover that, even now, after so many years, knowing she didn't know how to love him made her heart weep.

But she couldn't ignore the truth now, just as she

couldn't ignore it eight years ago. He'd deserved more than a flawed woman. He still did.

He made a deprecating sound. ''So you always said.''

Before she could ask him what he meant by that, his cell phone rang, shrill in the quiet of the lunchroom. He answered it and she chewed on a nail and went back to her thoughts, tuning out his conversation.

Once she thought about it, she really didn't want to know what his comment had meant. Their rocky past didn't matter anymore. What was done was done. She'd broken up with him, he'd taken off on his overseas adventure, and they'd both gone on.

And luckily for her, everything was different now. They didn't mean anything to each other anymore. New rules applied, thank the stars above.

Obviously Aiden hadn't figured that out yet. Like a bad case of déjà vu he wanted to peer inside her and *communicate* with her for the sake of the spread. Well, she wanted none of it.

Too bad.

She was stuck like a doomed bug on glue. And judging by the still-tingly skin on her arm and her shaking knees, taking Maggie along was absolutely necessary. Colleen needed some sort of shield from Aiden, and she intended that Maggie serve the part. She would make sure her neighbor stuck to her side every second of the weekend.

His voice interrupted her thoughts. ''That was the moving company. They're waiting at the house to deliver my stuff, so I've got to go.'' He moved to the door, jamming his tiny cell phone into the front pocket of his pants. ''We'll continue this conversation later.''

She rose and followed him, yanking her gaze from the front of his pants where he'd shoved his cell phone. She wanted to ask him where he lived and if he'd bought a new house. But she squashed the urge. For her own sanity and emotional safety she desperately needed to keep her distance from Aiden this time, not that he'd ever be interested in heating things up between them again.

''Aiden, wait.''

He stopped and turned, his green eyes questioning.

She ignored the sparks his gaze generated and gave him a hesitant smile. ''Can my friend and her baby come along?''

He reached out and squeezed her hand but his eyes remained cold. ''That depends on you.'' He let go of her, waved and left.

Score tied.

Aiden stepped outside and took a deep breath, filling his lungs with the warm summer air, liking the sound of the cars and buses zooming along. Though the offices of the *Beacon* were located in a building in the center of downtown Portland and lots of people and traffic hurried by, the sounds of a normal city, one not torn apart by bombs and war, calmed him. Thank God he was home. Even though he doubted he'd ever be safe from his devastating memories and scorching guilt, at least he was back in familiar territory, a place he could burrow into and fashion a new life.

Yeah, everything would be perfect if he didn't have to work with Colleen. But he did, and he wasn't going to let that fact bother him enough to ruin this job and his chance to obliterate the terrible memories burned in his mind.

Unbidden, images arose in his brain, images he was helpless to stop. Dying children. Grief-stricken parents. Hell on earth…

I did nothing.

He stopped, suddenly breathing heavily, sweat breaking out on his upper lip. Guilt roiled in his soul like boiling water, burning him little by little from the inside out.

He closed his eyes, and by sheer dint of will he forced the agonizing pictures away, the truth of the current situation with Colleen thudding down instead.

Take back the stupid deal.

Nodding, he did an about-face and headed back toward the offices of the *Beacon,* his memories putting his problem into instant perspective. Making any kind of deal with Colleen was idiotic. If she didn't want to work with him, fine. In fact, *better.* Easier. Less demanding. Less challenging.

He found Colleen sitting alone once again at a cluttered table in the lunchroom, staring off into space, a faraway, vulnerable expression on her face that unexpectedly landed like a kick in the gut. Fool. Why the hell should he care that she seemed sad? He ignored the unsettling sensation and cleared his throat. "Colleen."

Her gaze snapped to him. "Aiden." Surprise lit her cornflower-blue eyes. "Back so soon?"

"Yeah." He made a face when the scent of stinky, stale coffee grounds and burnt microwave popcorn assaulted his nose. But he'd take that smell any day over the stench of blood and death he'd never quite been able to banish.

He shook it off along with his bad memories and forced himself back on track, back to the present. "I'm calling off our deal."

She stood and stared at him, then pushed her hair back behind one ear and narrowed her eyes. "Why?"

"It's pretty simple, really," he said, irritated that he'd even considered making any kind of deal with Colleen, that he'd let her push him around. "All I want to do is take pictures of babies."

"Okay," she said, drawing the word out. "But what does this have to do with your...deal?"

He snorted. "I'm not going to make some dumb deal with you to make sure you find a way to work with me. That's your choice, not mine, and frankly, I don't give a damn what choice you make."

She widened her eyes, clearly taken aback by his harshness, then moved over and opened the refrigerator and pulled out a can of diet pop. "I don't know whether I should be jumping for joy or feel insulted."

He shrugged. "I'm not trying to be insulting, just realistic. I told myself that you needed to find a way to work with me to do this job." He let out a derisive laugh. "That's a load of bull, and I'm not going to beg you to do your job. I'm sure Joe can find someone else to work with me."

"Actually, I've already asked him to find someone and I'm it." She pulled her lips into a triumphant smile. "So I guess my friend and her baby are in."

He ground his back teeth together. It rubbed him the wrong way to have to redesign his layout to include another baby, but it wasn't worth fighting with Colleen about. The less contact he had with her, the better. He nodded. "Yeah, your friend and her baby are in."

Her face relaxed. "Good," she said, walking toward him. She laid her free hand on his forearm for a moment. "You won't regret it, I promise." She moved by, her scent briefly masking the coffee and popcorn smell. "I'm going to call Maggie right now. I bet she'll be thrilled."

Colleen left the lunchroom and Aiden felt the warm place her touch had branded on his arm. Her light scent lingered in the air, intoxicating and evocative, fueling memories of her in his arms, her blue eyes staring into his soul, making him feel happy and content and loved.

He snorted in disgust. Colleen had damn sure never, ever loved him. He quickly moved to the sink and pulled a paper cup from the dispenser on the wall next to the sink. He filled it with cold water from the tap and downed the cool liquid in one gulp.

Obviously, his memories of how wonderful and content she'd always made him feel were still vivid in his mind, rising up at the worst time to make him want her close to him all over again.

Get over it. He didn't want to remember how much he'd loved Colleen, how much he'd wanted to share his life with her, any more than he wanted to go beyond the bounds of a mildly cordial working relationship with her. She was a bundle of complications and inevitable heartache rolled into one woman.

No doubt about it. The man he'd become after photographing terrible scenes of death, destruction and poverty wanted nothing to do with Colleen. She was bad news, and as soon as he made it through their long weekend together and "The Baby Chronicles" was complete, he'd leave her behind.

And that couldn't be soon enough for him.

Chapter Three

Colleen pushed aside the pale blue curtains hanging on the sliding glass door of her and Maggie's rented condo at Sun Mountain. A breathtaking view of majestic Mount Bachelor to the south of the resort, framed by wispy clouds turned to vibrant orange, pink and purple by the stunning summer sunset, greeted her. Huge, spiky juniper and pine trees, silhouetted by the dusky glow of the setting sun, waved in a light evening breeze.

She slid the door open and inhaled the fresh air and smiled at the picture-perfect scene, thankful the warm summer day had cooled off enough to take the edge off the high-desert afternoon heat. Maybe tomorrow they could cool off in the resort's huge pool.

She turned from the darkening sky, remembering that she was here to work on "The Baby Chronicles," not lounge around the pool working on her tan. Her smile faded.

Aiden would be arriving tomorrow.

Gorgeous scenery or not, she had to focus on her goal—to spend as little time with him as possible.

Mission acknowledged.

A heavy knock sounded on the condo door.

Colleen swung around, wondering who their visitor could be. She stepped toward the small, tiled entryway, intending to answer the door. But frazzled-looking Maggie, who had been trying to put a fussy Laura down since they'd arrived twenty minutes ago, stepped out from the hall that led to the bedrooms, Laura crying in her arms. "I'll get it." She held out Laura toward Colleen. "Here. Maybe you can calm her down."

"Yeah, right," Colleen said under her breath. She hesitated, then awkwardly took the baby and held her at arm's length, not quite sure how to hold the squalling little girl. She'd taken care of her preteen foster brothers and sisters, but never a baby. "Uh, Maggie…"

Surprisingly, Laura instantly stopped crying and turned her wide, red-rimmed blue eyes toward Colleen. Her mouth quivered and then she gave Colleen a slobbery smile, revealing a lone tooth on her bottom gum.

Colleen's heart twisted painfully inside her and she wanted to set the adorable baby down and run away from that ache. Out of nowhere, her biological clock ticked in her head, in direct opposition to her long-standing desire to never have kids of her own. "Hey, Laura." She bent her arms and awkwardly propped the baby on her hip, then nervously began pacing in a circle. "Not sleepy, huh?"

Laura continued to stare at her, then reached up with her chubby little hand and patted Colleen's cheek. "Ba, ba, ba!" She shoved her finger in Colleen's nose.

"Whoa there, sweetie," Colleen said, pulling the baby's hand away. "Not a good place for your finger." She continued to walk around and swayed her upper body because Laura seemed to like it.

The feel of Laura's tiny body in her arms and her nonsensical babbling miraculously filled Colleen with a strange sense of calm. She'd been forced to take care of lots of other kids, bratty, mean kids who had convinced her that she never wanted to be a parent. But standing here with little Laura in her arms, an unexpected desire for a baby welled up inside, taking her off guard.

Through her own confused thoughts, she heard a familiar male voice. She hoped she'd misheard, but her hopes were dashed when Maggie pushed the door open wider to reveal Aiden standing on the other side in shorts, a tank top and running shoes, looking like a model in a running-apparel commercial.

Colleen stopped, squeezing Laura tighter to her hip, and looked up and down his body. Laura squawked and Colleen loosened her grip, still staring at Aiden.

Mercy. His lightly tanned, well-muscled, hairy legs—generously displayed by the skimpy running shorts he wore—were, quite simply, gorgeous. In a very masculine sort of way, of course. His loose, black basketball jersey exposed way too much of his hair-sprinkled, rippled chest, sculpted arms and broad shoulders. He smiled at Maggie, showing his straight, white teeth. The skin surrounding them crinkled appealingly at the corners.

Colleen fidgeted, moving from foot to foot, then forced herself to calm down.

Hey, big deal. So he was a nice-looking guy. She dated handsome, sexy men all the time. She wasn't about to let his hunky body bother her, right?

Even so, she decided to get herself a cold drink before she put that resolution to the test face-to-face. She hiked Laura up on her hip and put herself into motion, glancing at Aiden as she made a hasty exit from the living room.

She frowned, then backed up a few steps to peer around the doorjamb at Aiden. Laura patted Colleen's face and then grabbed her ear, fingering the fake-diamond studs Colleen always wore. She pulled the hand away and nuzzled the baby's face, enjoying Laura's baby-scented skin. "Hey, little girl, cut it out."

She stared at Aiden, once again noting the new lines around his eyes—from stress?—his almost-but-not-quite-gaunt face, and dark shadows lingering in the depths of his eyes, taking the tiniest edge off his smile. Her frown still in place, she started moving again and stepped into the kitchen, a bubble of curiosity mixed with concern expanding in her brain.

Why did Aiden look so...changed? He'd always been a happy-go-lucky kind of guy, the kind who never had shadows darkening his gaze, whose smile was always brilliant and genuine. Biting her lip, her eyebrows knitted together, she went to the refrigerator and pulled out a two-liter container of diet pop with her free hand, then went looking for a glass, her mind stuck on the small, perplexing differences she'd seen in Aiden.

She hiked Laura up on her hip again and looked at the wide-eyed baby. "He looks different, Laura. What do you think about that?"

"Ba, ba, ba!" Laura replied around her slobbery fist.

"That pretty much sums it up." Colleen found a glass and was in the process of pouring herself a stout serving of cold pop when Maggie walked into the kitchen. Aiden trailed right behind her.

"You hiding in here?" Maggie asked, her brown eyes alight with curiosity.

Colleen gripped the glass and pressed her mouth into what she hoped was a relaxed smile. "Of course not." She looked at Aiden, her nerves ratcheting up a notch. "Hey, Aiden. Arrive a little early?"

He nodded, his gaze lingering on the baby in her arms. "Colleen," he said in a clipped voice, his jaw flexing. "I got away earlier than I expected."

For some reason, his frosty greeting created a dull hole in the pit of her stomach, although she shouldn't be surprised by his cold tone after her rude behavior the afternoon he'd come to the *Beacon*.

Or after she'd broken up with him.

She pretended the chasm in her belly didn't exist, determined to follow the tradition her parents had turned into an art form before they'd dumped her on the steps of the Children's Services Department, and act as if everything was just peachy.

She cast her gaze to Maggie, intending to fall back on old-fashioned etiquette and make small talk and introductions. "Maggie, this is Aiden Forbes—"

"Oh, we met at the door." Maggie took Laura, who had gone back to inspecting Colleen's earrings, from her. "I recognized him right away from your *description*." She waggled her eyebrows.

Colleen threw Maggie a furtive glare and fought back the urge to whack her on the shoulder. Granted, Colleen had gushed a bit over Aiden's fantastic looks, but she certainly didn't want Maggie to share that information with him. Colleen was going to be necessarily detached and uninvolved now, not hot and heavy.

"Oh, okay," Colleen said innocuously.

Maggie stepped around Colleen to pull two more glasses from the cupboard. "Listen, Aiden's going for a run, but I invited him for a late dinner afterward." She smiled brightly. "Is that all right?"

Colleen's heart sank like a brick. Maggie was supposed to be her buffer not her social planner. She gave Maggie a thanks-a-lot look.

Aiden and Maggie stared at her, waiting for an answer, Maggie's eyes alight with mischief, Aiden's sea-green and challenging. Was he was waiting for Colleen to throw a hissy fit?

While her first instinct *was* to yell *not on your life!,* she'd promised herself that she was going to stay balanced this weekend *no matter what,* and that included, very unfortunately, unexpected dinners with Aiden and scheming friends. No hissy fits allowed.

She smiled broadly and said, "Great." Even though it wasn't.

Aiden raised an eyebrow. "You're sure?"

Colleen took a sip of pop. "Sure I'm sure. Why wouldn't I be?"

He planted his large hands on his hips and lifted one big, bulging shoulder, then threw a quick glance to Maggie. "Oh, no reason," he said significantly.

He turned his attention to Laura, his face softening. He held out a finger to her. "Hey, cutie-pie." The baby grabbed on to him for a moment, slobber running down her chin. He leaned down and said some nonsense words to Laura, eliciting a smile from her.

Colleen stared at Aiden and the baby, her breath stalled, her chest tightening. She yanked her gaze from the endearing sight, thankful when Maggie mumbled under her breath about a stinky diaper and left the room with Laura.

Colleen drew in a deep, calming breath, set her glass on the simple pine table and started unloading the groceries. "You're welcome to stay if you want to, just don't expect anything fancy."

"Hey, I'm a guy. I survived on Cup O'Noodles in college. Although I seem to remember you were a mean cook.'' He stepped closer and craned his neck to look into the grocery bag. ''What's on the menu?''

His compliment pleased her, as did his positive memories of her cooking skills, the only thing remotely domestic she was any good at. Unfortunately, being pleased by his approval was bad, almost as bad as his clean, wood-laced scent tantalizing her nose, and his male, partially bare body looming over her, making her sweat. ''Roasted veggies, chicken and pasta.'' She stepped back, a package of pasta in her hand, suppressing the dumb urge to press her nose to his chest and breathe deep.

And lose herself in his arms and the tender words he'd always whispered in her ear.

''Sounds a heck of a lot better than the cheese and crackers I'd planned.'' He looked at his sports watch. ''What time do we eat?''

Colleen squatted and opened a cupboard, searching for a saucepan. ''In an hour,'' she said, wishing he wasn't going to be hanging around all evening, making mincemeat of her control, raising inane questions in her mind about what had happened to put the new shadows in his eyes.

Turning, he moved toward the door to the kitchen, already working up to a jog.

''Aiden, wait.'' She rose and bit her lip.

He stopped and turned around. ''Yeah?''

''Is everything all right?'' she blurted.

He stared at her, his green eyes darkening to the shade of pine trees at night. He blinked and a blank nothingness appeared in his gaze. "Everything's fine." He looked away, then back. "Why?"

She shrugged, wishing she hadn't given in to her stupid curiosity. "I don't know. You seem… different."

He pressed his mouth into a hard, tight line. "I'm fine." He backed away. "I'll be back in an hour." He turned and left the condo, the screen door slamming in his wake.

Colleen drew in a deep breath and let it out. She might not have had a clue about how to love him so many years ago, but she *had* known how to read him, and had always been able to tell when something was wrong.

He'd lied.

She'd seen it in his suddenly vacant eyes and in the tight, clammed-up expression he'd worn.

Maggie's voice interrupted her wandering thoughts. "Whoa, baby. Your description, as stunning as it was, doesn't begin to do him justice. That is one good-looking guy."

Colleen stood frozen, saucepan in hand, and shook her head, hoping to shake thoughts of Aiden from her brain and gain some sanity along the way. "Tell me about it." She turned and glared at Maggie. "And what do you think you're doing?"

Maggie widened her brown eyes, her expression all innocence. "I have no idea what you're talking about."

Colleen made a rude noise, grabbed a package of baby carrots and ruthlessly attacked the plastic covering. "Yeah, right, Little Miss Matchmaker." She poked a finger toward Maggie. "You set me up."

Maggie snagged a baby carrot from the package and nibbled. "Oh, relax. What's the big deal? You said he was just an old friend."

"Old boyfriend," Colleen corrected, reaching for a paring knife she'd found earlier. "There's a big difference."

"Maybe. And maybe I did set you up. But what's wrong with that? He's an absolute dream, Colleen. You should go for it."

Colleen very deliberately set the knife down and turned around. "Let's get one thing straight, all right?" She drilled Maggie with a pointed gaze. "Aiden and I are history. Over with. I'm not going to *go for it* with him. Ever." No way would she let herself believe, even for a moment, that her flaw had suddenly disappeared, miraculously gifting her with the ability to be loved and return the emotion.

Maggie gazed at Colleen speculatively. "Why not? Things change."

No. Nothing had changed. She was still the same old flawed Colleen, the one her parents hadn't wanted.

Her eyes suddenly stinging, she resumed chopping. "Aiden and I aren't getting back together, Maggie," she said, swallowing the lump in her throat. "Obviously you've forgotten that I told you I wanted you to come here with me so I wouldn't have to spend any time with him." She shoved the cut carrots off the cutting board into a plastic bowl. "So let's just drop this, all right?"

Before Maggie could reply, Laura cried out. Maggie rolled her eyes. "Fine. I'll drop it." She turned to leave the kitchen. "But only because I need to go check on Laura. I hope she sleeps tonight." She pressed a hand to her lower stomach, winced and bent over. "Oh, man, I don't feel too well."

Colleen walked over and placed a hand on Maggie's shoulder. "You all right?"

"Probably just that gut-bomb burger I ate for lunch today." Maggie straightened. "I'll be fine."

Colleen stood immobile after Maggie left the room, the paring knife in her hand, her watery eyes clearing, hoping that Maggie's vacation weekend wouldn't be ruined by illness. This was the first chance Maggie had had to get away since her husband had walked out on her and Laura six months ago, shortly after Laura had been born, claiming he couldn't handle the stress of a child.

Colleen started chopping again, hoping to lose herself in the calming, repetitive motion that usually relaxed her.

It didn't work. Inevitably, a picture of Aiden, complete with endearing, crooked smile and sparkling eyes, materialized. His smile had always made her knees weak, and his eyes had always seemed as if they could see deep into her soul.

She shivered.

Her soul was still off limits.

And now, thanks to dear old Maggie, Aiden would

be returning in an hour to have dinner with them, darn it.

She wanted to stay away from Aiden, not hang out with him. Or wonder about the new shadows in his eyes and the faint, tug-on-her-heart hardness in his jaw. Or have to watch him with Laura.

Or wish herself back into his arms, no matter how much she'd loved being there.

But she'd vowed to get through this weekend with grace and a minimum of fuss, and she would. She would smile and talk and treat Aiden as if he was just an old friend instead of the only man who had ever turned her world upside down, the only person on the face of the earth who had ever come close to opening up her heart.

She absolutely, positively refused to repeat history.

After a five-mile run on the multitude of paved paths meandering around Sun Mountain, Aiden cooled down and returned to his condo for a shower. He dressed quickly in blue Nike shorts and white T-shirt, wondering if he was an idiot for having dinner with Colleen and Maggie.

Colleen's questions an hour ago had raised red flags all over the place. He didn't want her probing at painful things he couldn't talk about. Maybe it was her reporter's instincts at work.

Whatever it was, he'd have to be on guard. His wounds were none of her business, even though she was responsible for some of them.

And hers were none of his, though he was having

a hard time forgetting Colleen's uncharacteristically messy office, dead plants and all, and the new sort of vulnerability he'd noticed in her eyes. She'd always been so strong, so invincible, and so with it.

So damn independent.

He clenched his hands into fists, shoving aside the razor-sharp memories of her jamming a knife into his heart, memories of Colleen leaving him and what that had led to—dying babies, suffering children.

His failure.

Dammit. He couldn't let himself dwell on what haunted him—Colleen's desertion, his hellish years overseas, both strangely connected—if he was to make it through this weekend unscathed.

He left his condo and walked the short distance to Colleen and Maggie's unit, his thoughts snagging on how gorgeous Colleen had looked almost an hour ago in her tight pink tank top, flat sandals and denim shorts that displayed her shapely, tan legs to perfection.

Despite his recent cool shower, unwanted heat built in his body.

Good thing he could deal with that.

Although the tantalizing domestic picture he'd gotten a load of when he'd walked into the kitchen and seen her with that baby in her arms wasn't so easy to deal with or forget. For an achy second he'd remembered how he'd once dreamed of Colleen holding *their* baby.

Gotta let that go, too.

When he arrived at their door, he paused for a moment, reminding himself that he was simply looking forward to a good homemade meal and some innocuous conversation. Besides, Maggie would make what might have been an intimate dinner with Colleen an unthreatening threesome.

Straightforward. Simple. Uncomplicated. A harmless way for the weekend to start off. No way was he going to fall for Colleen again. No way in hell.

He knocked on the door and Colleen answered a few moments later, without the cute baby in her arms. She smiled shyly at him—the first genuine smile she'd given him since he'd seen her three days ago—flashing the adorable dimples he'd always loved to kiss.

She shoved her hands in the back pockets of her shorts. "Hey."

He forced himself to smile back, despite the way her shy smile made it hard for him to breathe. "Hey yourself."

She continued to stare at him, moving restlessly from foot to foot. If he didn't know better, he would swear she was feeling bashful. Which was ridiculous. Colleen was a lot of things, but bashful wasn't on the list. She'd always been an outgoing party animal. Staying put hadn't been her forte.

He stared back, waiting for her to invite him in. When she didn't, he nodded toward the door and said, "Are we going to eat out here?"

Her cheeks colored. "Of course not." She ducked her head and yanked open the door and stepped aside.

"I don't know what I was thinking," she said under her breath.

Aiden stepped past her, detecting the faint scent that always hovered in the air around her. Man, how he'd loved the way she smelled like fresh, juicy peaches on a warm summer day. And damn, if he hadn't always packed canned peaches whenever he had to travel somewhere awful. Comfort food if he'd ever had it.

Shoving that disturbing thought aside, he stepped past the entrance to the kitchen on the right and moved into the living room. The small room was adorned with condo-standard, neutral-colored rattan furniture, a small television and ugly prints of flowers on the walls. The blue drapes on the sliding door had been flung wide to reveal a low-slung moon glowing in the star-studded evening sky.

Colleen stepped into the living room. "Look, there's been a slight hitch. Maggie's not feeling well, and I had to help her with the baby, so I haven't had time to finish making dinner."

Concerned, he asked, "What's wrong?"

She rolled her eyes and smoothed back a stray curl. "Matchmaking."

"Excuse me?"

She pulled her mouth into an uneasy-looking smile. "I know this is ridiculous, but I think she's pretending she's sick so you and I will be—" her face pinkened "—alone."

He roamed his gaze over her becoming, blush-tinged cheeks. "Ah," he said, even though he didn't really understand. "Why would she want to do that?"

Colleen lifted a slender shoulder. "She's got this crazy idea that you and I, well…that we…um, might get back together."

He stared at her, slack-jawed.

She quickly held up a hand, nodding. "Don't worry, she'll soon see that us getting together is a totally ridiculous, dumb idea. But I think she's decided to put it to the test."

He couldn't agree more. Maggie's matchmaking, while sort of endearing, was a waste of time, not to mention as far-fetched as a cat that barked. He'd never let Colleen work her way into his heart again. "So, what's the plan?"

She cast her gaze down the hall, then looked back at him, her eyes troubled. "I don't know. She's being pretty stubborn. I guess I'm going to try and talk her out of this whole thing." A crease formed between her dark blond eyebrows. "Do you mind waiting?"

He held up his hands. "Have at it. I know any dinner you cook will be worth waiting for." He might want to forget how she'd cut out his heart, but he definitely remembered how much he'd enjoyed her cooking.

She smiled slowly, spreading her lightly glossed lips wide, looking pleased by his compliment. "Why, thank you, kind sir," she said, inclining her head, her blue eyes, framed by feathery, dark lashes, sparkling like a crystal-clear South Seas ocean in sunlight. "I'll be back in a few minutes—with Maggie."

Her genuine smile stole his breath away as easily as a pickpocket in Italy had once swiped his wallet. Struggling to drag in a breath, he watched her leave the living room and walk down the short hallway toward the bedrooms, remembering how her smile had always melted his heart and made him feel like the luckiest man on earth. It was hard to forget how he'd always felt as if he was exactly where he was supposed to be when she was near, how happy she'd made him, at least for a while.

And damned if he didn't want to stride down the hall, pull her into his arms and lose himself in the sense of belonging and absolute contentment that no other woman had ever made him feel.

A stupid, emotionally suicidal wish if he ever had one.

Colleen took a deep, calming breath, trying to regain her wayward sanity before stepping into the bedroom Maggie and Laura shared. She was determined to get to the bottom of Maggie's sudden, seemingly convenient illness.

A low moan sounded in the room.

A ripple of concern ran down Colleen's spine. That sound seemed to be more than just a little good-natured playacting. She bit her lip and cast an interested gaze to Laura, who was happily playing with a rattle in the portable playpen Maggie had brought along. The precious baby was now bundled in a pink cotton shorts outfit with puppies embroidered on the front, her chubby, bare legs kicking in the air while she shook the rattle. She turned and looked right at Colleen and gurgled and smiled in recognition.

Colleen's heart twisted into a hard knot in her chest. Holding back a gasp, she deliberately yanked her gaze from Laura, determined not to yearn for something she wouldn't know how to love.

She walked toward the bed where Maggie lay on her side, curled into a little ball. "Maggie," she said, bending near. "How are you feeling?"

Maggie rolled her head on the pillow to look at Colleen, her face devoid of color. Pain shone in the depths of her dull eyes. "Not so good." A visible shiver moved through her. "Bad cramps. They hurt."

Colleen reached out and laid a palm on Maggie's forehead. The skin was very hot and dry to the touch. She tamped down the panic rising in her. Maggie had spiked a fever in the last hour.

This was no ruse.

Colleen sat on the edge of the bed, feeling ashamed for even thinking that Maggie was faking an illness to throw Colleen and Aiden together. "Where's the pain? Right side or left?"

"Right," Maggie said on a low, agonized groan. She turned and looked at Colleen with tears shimmering in her eyes. "It's really bad."

Colleen squeezed Maggie's shoulder. "Any nausea?"

"A little."

"Relax. I'll take care of you." She stood, her mind racing, reviewing Maggie's symptoms. Intense abdominal pain. A fever. Nausea.

A sense of dread crept over Colleen.

She remembered the appendicitis she'd had ten years ago during her freshman year in college. She wasn't a doctor, but Maggie's symptoms seemed the same.

Maggie moaned again and clutched her hands to her lower belly. "I think I need a doctor."

Decision made. Colleen glanced at her watch: 9:00 p.m. Too late for a regular doctor's office. Maybe Sun Mountain had an urgent-care facility.

"I'll be right back." She quickly moved out of the room and down the hall, telling herself to remain calm.

Aiden was sitting on the couch, reading a local sight-seeing magazine the resort had provided. The moment he saw her hurrying down the hall, he stood, drilling her with an intense, concerned gaze. "What's wrong?"

She went straight for the phone. "Maggie's not faking." She punched zero for the resort operator. "She's really sick. I think she might have appendicitis."

Aiden came to stand by her side, his green eyes alight with worry, while she had a brief but illuminating conversation with the concierge desk at the resort's main hotel. When she was finished and had the information she needed, she hung up and looked at Aiden, suddenly glad he was here to help her through this.

"The resort's urgent care closed at 5:00 p.m. The nearest medical care is in Bend." She took a deep, shaky breath. "I could drive her there, but I'm not sure that's a good idea. It's a thirty-minute ride, it's dark, and I don't even know where Saint Charles Hospital is." She bit her lip, torn about how best to take care of Maggie. "She's in a lot of pain, and I'm thinking an ambulance could get here faster..." She looked at him. "Hey, did you have some sort of medical training overseas?"

His eyes darkened. "Not really, but I did deal with some injuries. You want me to take a look at her?"

She tugged on her bottom lip with her teeth and nodded.

"Okay." He moved in the direction of Maggie's room, gesturing for Colleen to follow.

She followed, her legs shaking.

When she stepped into the room, Aiden was sitting on the bed, holding Maggie's hand, talking to her in soothing, calm tones. Maggie, looking paler and weaker and in intense pain, responded listlessly between moans. He pressed a hand to her forehead and nodded his head.

Without preamble, he said, "I think you're right, Colleen." He turned and gave Colleen a grim look, his eyes as dark as the forest at night. "We should get her to a doctor right away. Call 911." He smoothed Maggie's hair back. "I'll stay with her."

Colleen nodded, touched by and thankful for Aiden's gentleness and his levelheaded support. She spun on her heel and left the room, an anxious, sick lump of foreboding moving through her like a ball of acid. She prayed Maggie would be all right.

She grabbed the phone and dialed 911. When the operator answered, Colleen told her what was wrong and gave her their location in as calm a manner as she could manage. The operator asked some questions about Maggie's symptoms, which Colleen promptly answered, and then the operator instructed her to stay on the line until the paramedics arrived.

While Colleen waited, she drummed a pencil on the counter, her mind spinning like a top inside her head. She desperately hoped, for Maggie's sake, that Maggie's illness was nothing more serious than a simple case of the flu or a stomach bug or food poisoning.

Another thought zapped through her mind like an electric shock. If Maggie did have appendicitis, she would need surgery.

And while Colleen would gladly do whatever necessary to help Maggie out, if Maggie was in the hospital, Colleen would be alone. With Aiden and an adorable baby. Two things she'd sworn to avoid for her entire adult life. Two people who had the proved power to make her ache and bleed inside.

Mercy.

Chapter Four

The next morning, Colleen hung up the phone and looked at Laura, long over feeling the urge to weep every time she laid eyes on the munchkin. "Your mommy says hi."

The baby gurgled and picked up a handful of rice cereal and flung it on the floor with a plop. "Ba!"

Talk about trial by fire. Colleen slumped her shoulders and looked dolefully at Laura, exhausted from a long, sleepless night spent attending to a fussy baby who hadn't had any intention of actually sleeping in a strange place for more than an hour or two at a time.

Now, to top it all off, the exasperating little angel was covered from head to toe in gooey, sticky rice cereal. Did any of the food actually get eaten? Maggie had said not to worry, that Laura wouldn't let herself starve, but Colleen had to wonder.

"Ba, ba, ba!" Laura squealed, flailing the spoon she had clutched in her chubby little fist in the air. More cereal flew in every direction and a gigantic glob landed right in the middle of Colleen's forehead.

"Nice shot." Colleen made a face as she wiped away the lump of lukewarm cereal with a napkin. She'd tried to hold the spoon and feed Laura, which would have undoubtedly been a heck of a lot neater, not to mention more nutritious, but Laura would have none of that. She simply opened her mouth and howled—the child had lovely tonsils—until Colleen surrendered the spoon. Apparently, Laura was really, really into feeding herself, although Colleen used "feeding" in the very loosest sense of the word. "Cereal flinging" would be more appropriate.

Colleen wearily wiped a hand through her own sticky, cereal-encrusted hair, eyeing the baby. How in the world was an inexperienced, totally clueless woman like herself going to deal with the overwhelming responsibility Maggie's sudden appendicitis had dumped in her lap?

Yes, sirree, Colleen's fear of being left alone to care for Laura had been realized, and her amateur, totally unscientific appendicitis diagnosis had turned out to be right on the money. The paramedics had arrived shortly after her 911 call. They'd listened to a rundown of Maggie's symptoms, done an exam, loaded her up and whisked her to the hospital for an emergency appendectomy. Colleen had wanted to accompany her friend, and Aiden had even offered to go to the hospital, but Maggie had insisted they stay behind to take care of Laura. Maybe Maggie had known that it would take two adults to keep up with the champion cereal flinger.

Colleen hadn't argued with Maggie, even though the thought of spending so much one-on-one time with Laura had filled her with a strange combination of stark fear and an unexplained, totally unexpected sense of anticipation. How could she ever hope to keep her growing yearning for a baby of her own under control when she had to take care of an irresistible, cereal-bedecked cherub like Laura?

But Colleen would dutifully step up to the plate and take care of Laura for the next day or two, until Maggie was released from the hospital. Maggie was depending on her, and Colleen wasn't about to let her friend down. Although Colleen had wanted to run screaming into the night when she'd bravely attacked the task of changing the nuclear waste masquerading as a dirty diaper this morning—twice. Obviously, lots and lots of food had at some point made it in.

After her long, sleepless, totally exhausting night, Colleen realized that she might have been a bit hasty when she'd insisted Aiden go back to his own condo after Maggie had been taken away by the paramedics. Another adult around probably would have been a godsend. But all Colleen had been able to think about late last night was that dealing with Laura was going to be hard enough without adding tempting, nerve-racking Aiden into the mix.

She glanced at her watch. Nine-twenty. "Whoa, little girl. We're due outside at the front fountain for the shoot in forty minutes." She looked at Laura, then looked down at herself at the globs of cereal sticking to the oversize T-shirt and shorts she'd slept in. She curled her lip and shook her head. "We are one huge cereal mess, you know that? Guess we better clean up."

Colleen went over to the counter and ripped off a huge length of paper towel. She was in the process of trying to pick the cereal from Laura's wispy hair (and having very little luck with the gluey problem) when a knock sounded on the front door.

Frowning, Colleen put the hunk of paper towel down on the pine kitchen table and moved toward the front door.

Laura screamed bloody murder and held out her arms.

Colleen hightailed it back to her. "Okay, okay, you can come." She tried to pry the spoon from Laura's hand, but the baby howled and jerked her hand away. "All right, keep it," Colleen muttered, then unhooked Laura from the high chair Maggie had brought along, lifted the baby out and propped her on her hip. Together, they hurried to the door.

Aiden stood on the other side, dressed in jeans, a green T-shirt that matched his eyes and an Oregon Ducks baseball cap. A totally ridiculous sense of relief moved through Colleen. She blurted, "Boy am I glad to see you."

His eyebrows shot up.

Rationalizing her relief, she explained, "It'll be nice to be with someone who can walk, talk, eat and go potty by himself."

He kicked up one side of his mouth, then moved his gaze over her and Laura's cereal-decorated selves. He frowned quizzically. To Colleen's astonishment, he reached out and stroked his fingers across her cheek, caressing her in a way that made her heart race and lit tiny, hot fires under the skin where he'd touched her. She had to resist the urge to nuzzle his hand with her face.

He brought his hand away and looked at the piece of cereal goo he'd wiped off her face, then looked back up, mirth dancing in his eyes. "What happened to you two? Did a cereal factory explode?"

Colleen glared at him, unaccountably disappointed that he'd been removing cereal rather than touching her for touching's sake. "Ha, ha." She swung away, intending to go back into the kitchen to work on Laura's hair. She looked back over her shoulder. "Do you have any idea how difficult it is to feed a baby?"

He stepped inside, closed the door and followed her to the kitchen. "I'm the oldest of five, Colleen. I was feeding babies when I was ten years old."

She picked up the paper towel and went back to work. "That's the problem. She won't let *me* feed her. She wants to do it herself, although, as you can see, she didn't eat much." She gestured to the cereal-covered floor and table.

Aiden stood in the doorway to the kitchen, his

hands propped on his hips, watching her. "What are you doing?"

She shot him an irritated look. "What does it look like? I'm cleaning her hair."

He moved toward her, shaking his head. "You'll never get all that cereal out that way. It sticks like glue. She needs a bath."

Colleen widened her eyes and blinked. "Oh." She bit her lip, feeling woefully inadequate. "I have no idea how to give a baby a bath."

He took the paper towel from her. "It's not rocket science. I'll show you how."

Colleen wasn't sure she liked the sound of that. Spending any time alone with Aiden and Laura, doing domestic, mother/father/baby kinds of activities was sure to remind her that the empty space in her heart would see to it that she would never have a baby or husband of her own.

She plucked the paper towel from his hands. "No, thank you. I'll manage this way." She glanced at her watch. "Oh, rats. I still have to shower before the shoot starts—"

"Actually, that's why I'm here. It's raining. I've postponed everything until the weather clears."

Colleen stared at Aiden, her stomach falling. She'd been looking forward to the shoot, even though it would mean working with Aiden, simply because she wanted to get out of the condo and interact with other adults. "I haven't had a spare second to look outside." She headed across the living room and flung open the blue drapes.

A gray, cloud-filled sky greeted her. Driving rain fell in sheets and a stiff breeze blew through the juniper trees, causing their branches to sway back and forth. The high desert sun was nowhere to be seen. Definitely not a day for photographs. Darn.

She turned around and looked back at Aiden. "Bad luck, huh?"

He shrugged. "Hey, it's part of taking photos outside. Sometimes the weather doesn't cooperate. Some clouds are good, but rain and wind—no way."

She gave him a half smile and yawned. "I was kind of looking forward to a change in scenery—and a break."

"Did you sleep at all last night?" He moved closer, surprising concern evident in his eyes.

"Not much," she admitted, liking his obvious worry just a little too much. Nothing but trouble down that path. She shifted Laura to her other hip and moved away, maintaining space. "I don't know how Maggie does all of this on her own."

"Parenting is hard work."

She eyed Laura. The baby was gumming the spoon to death. "I've discovered that. I'm in way over my head here."

"Well, you're in luck then," he announced. "I may be out of practice, but I've had lots of experience with babies. My mom had me helping with my younger siblings all the time."

"I don't know…" She trailed off, again debating the wisdom of allowing Aiden to help her out. While she certainly could use any help she could get, how smart was it to have Aiden around all day long, getting under her skin, making her uncomfortable?

Before she could make sense of her thoughts, another wave of exhaustion rolled through her. Suddenly, Laura weighed a ton. Needing to sit, Colleen moved to the couch. Laura dropped the spoon on the way and immediately began to cry.

Colleen sank down on the couch and smelled something foul. Again? Incredulous, she looked at a screaming, red-faced Laura and stood. "You, little girl, are a genuine poop machine."

Laura chose that exact moment to spit up whatever small amount of cereal had actually made it into her system. Thank heaven the child was wearing a disposable bib.

Unfortunately, Colleen was not.

Making a face, she looked down at the patch of goo on her shoulder, then made an instant decision. Even though she wasn't anywhere near eager to spend the day with Aiden, she had learned to be practical, and she was way out of her element. She needed help. Badly.

She held Laura at arm's length and looked at Aiden, giving him a wan smile. "Is that offer for help still open?"

He hesitated, and for a moment looked as if he wasn't going to agree. But then he smiled back, sort of, bent down and picked up the spoon, wiped it off on his shirt and handed it to Laura. "You bet."

Laura didn't stop crying, even though she had her prized spoon back in her hand. Colleen murmured some nonsense words in the baby's ear, trying to calm her down, all the while breathing an unexpected sigh of relief that she'd have some help for a little while.

Surely dealing with a fussy baby would be easier with another adult around, even if that adult was Aiden.

But in some far-off corner of her brain, another thought occurred to her.

Was she trading one kind of trouble for another?

For some reason, the sight of Colleen standing with a screaming Laura in her arms, both of them covered in cereal, warmed Aiden's heart in a way he'd never felt before today. In fact, his heart had been pretty darn toasty, dammit, ever since he'd seen no-nonsense, party-animal Colleen standing at the front door holding Laura on her hip, the picture of frazzled domesticity, looking as if she'd slogged through baby hell all night long.

Obviously, she didn't have a clue about babies.

And that was the only reason he'd offered to help at all. He felt sorry for Colleen; she'd been shoved into an unfamiliar, difficult situation. Helping out had absolutely nothing to do with playing daddy to Colleen's reluctant mommy, and he could certainly spend part of a day here without letting himself get sucked into Colleen's allure again, right?

Determined to make himself useful, he reached out and plucked a wailing Laura from Colleen's arms. The baby stopped crying and gazed at him. Blessed silence reigned in the condo.

Colleen drew in her chin and stood, shaking her head. "I guess you have the magic touch."

He smiled, pleased by her compliment, and shrugged. "Hey, kids like me. Now how about that lesson on bathing babies?"

Colleen picked a glob of dried cereal from her hair and gestured to the spit-up on her shoulder. "Would you mind if I showered first?"

"Oh, sure," he said, propping Laura on his forearm. "Show me the diapering supplies and I'll take care of the stinkpot." He pressed a quick kiss to a clean spot on Laura's cheek.

Laura jerked away and looked at him, her lower lip quivering. Huge tears formed in her eyes. Her face reddened. Her body stiffened. And then she opened her mouth and started howling again.

As he vaguely wondered how something so small could make such an earsplitting sound, Colleen walked by and patted his arm. "Guess the magic touch is gone, huh?"

Deflated, he moved his arm up and down to soothe Laura. She screamed louder. "We'll get along just fine, won't we?" he asked Laura.

Colleen waved a hand in the air and walked down the hall. "Whatever you say. Follow me."

He trailed along behind Colleen down the hall to Maggie's room. On one side was what could only be described as the diaper-bag explosion site. Clean disposable diapers, baby wipes, a tube of diaper-rash ointment and numerous other baby-changing items, including several extra baby undershirts, lay scattered all over half of the room.

He shook his head. "I guess there was more than one explosion here this morning," he loudly said over Laura's crying, eyeing the mess.

Colleen glared sideways at him. "I did the best I could given that I'd never even changed a diaper until last night."

"Well, I've changed plenty. Go take your shower and I'll deal with this." He held Laura up.

Colleen practically sprinted out of the room.

With practiced ease, he laid Laura on the floor, unbuttoned her stretchy pajamas and changed her diaper, marveling at how much easier it was to deal with a disposable diaper rather than the cloth diapers his mom had always used on his younger siblings.

Laura continued to rant, even through his rousing rendition of "Old Macdonald Had a Farm," complete with barnyard sounds, which had always worked on his brothers and sisters.

She was one tough customer.

Laura's screams brought back to mind all the starving, crying, inconsolable babies he'd seen while working overseas. Predictably, an icy shudder skated up his spine. Was there such a thing as a serene baby? He wanted—needed—to take pictures of happy, cooing, placid babies. What if he didn't find one? What then? The disturbing question lodged in his brain.

He finished changing Laura and went to work turning her into a peaceful baby. But over the next half hour, it became increasingly evident that there was no

such thing as the magic touch where Laura was concerned. She cried constantly.

By the time Colleen came out, freshly showered
and dressed in jeans and a short-sleeved, light blue
T-shirt that matched her eyes, he was at his wit's end
and Laura's screams had taken on a frantic, desperate
tone.

The moment Laura spotted Colleen, she held out
her arms and howled.

Colleen stopped dead in the middle of the living
room, her eyes wide, clearly astonished that Laura
wanted her.

That disbelieving look hit him hard, giving him an
unwanted, disconcerting glimpse into Colleen's vulnerability. It would be so much easier to keep her at
arm's length without seeing her doubts about herself
written all over her face. "I guess you're it." He
walked over and plopped the scream machine into
Colleen's arms. He gave her a wry smile. "Apparently I'm *not* the one with the magic touch."

Laura instantly stopped crying, nuzzled her red,
tear-stained face in the space between Colleen's neck
and shoulder, and then turned and glared at him as if
he was The Big Bad Wolf.

After a moment of stunned inaction, Colleen responded like a natural. She cupped the back of
Laura's curl-topped head and planted a kiss on the
baby's forehead. "It's okay, honey. I've got you
now."

She turned away and began to walk around the living room, gently swaying back and forth, crooning

soft words into Laura's ear. She moved to the couch and lowered herself, adjusting Laura on the way down so the baby was lying in her arms. Laura let out a shuddering, noisy breath and relaxed, then reached up to finger Colleen's earrings. Colleen smiled dreamily at her and smoothed Laura's sticky curls back.

Aiden stared at the two of them, unable to look away from the tender picture before him, despite his common sense screaming at him. A strange feeling hit hard, a chest-tightening sensation that filled him with warmth and clogged the breath in his throat.

The two of them looked as if they belonged together, looked like the most natural pair on the face of the earth.

What? How had Colleen morphed from the self-absorbed, emotionally barren woman he'd always known into this picture of loving, motherly perfection?

A strange uneasiness dropped like a lead weight in his belly. He didn't want to imagine Colleen in positive terms.

It sure looked as though Colleen had the baby situation under control, and he needed some air and distance from the endearing scene unfolding in front of him. He liked this new side of Colleen too damn much when he didn't want to like her at all. He wanted, needed, to think of her as the woman who'd hurt him rather than as a real, vulnerable person.

''Uh, well, looks like you're doing fine,'' he said, backing up, noticing that Laura was dropping off to sleep, obviously exhausted by her crying jag. "I'll just go now."

"No!" Colleen whispered loudly, glancing down at Laura, who slept on. "I mean, well, you know, she still needs a bath, and I really don't want to take that on by myself."

He stopped, torn between wanting to escape his strange thoughts and wanting to help her.

Before he could respond, Colleen smiled hopefully. "Please stay. I may have this under control now, but I'm sure this lull is just temporary. She won't sleep long, and I could really use some backup when she wakes up."

Knowing Colleen, she must be pretty desperate to actually ask for his help, and he'd never been the type to walk out on a damsel in distress. He'd just have to be sure not to dwell on how sweet and right and perfect she and Laura looked together.

On how much Colleen might have changed.

What he needed to remember was her MO: Make a man care. Cut out. Break his heart. If he kept that sobering reality in mind, he should have no trouble hanging around.

He let out a heavy breath, vaguely wondering if he'd lost his common sense, despite his rather plausible rationalization for staying. "Okay, I'll stay for a while. Would you like some breakfast?"

"You read my mind," she quietly said. "How about one of those killer omelettes you used to make?"

"Coming right up." He turned and walked into the

kitchen, remembering how often he'd made omelettes for Colleen—one of the many hoops he'd jumped through for her pleasure.

And he tried not to think about one single, unsettling thought: realistically, ignoring how real and perfect Colleen looked with the baby probably wasn't going to be as easy as it sounded. Even though he'd convinced himself that her past romantic sins had made him impervious to her, the disturbing truth was this new, improved version of Colleen intrigued the hell out of him.

Chapter Five

Praying that Laura wouldn't wake up, Colleen tiptoed out of Maggie's room. Thank goodness the little stinker was dead to the world from her crying fit and lack of sleep the night before. Colleen desperately needed a short break from the exhausting job of caring for a fussy, screaming infant.

Running a hand through her still-damp hair, Colleen breathed a sigh of relief when she made it to the hall and didn't hear a peep from Laura. Hopefully she would sleep long enough for Colleen to recharge her battery by eating breakfast.

With Aiden.

Oh, mercy. Aiden was here, the man who had turned her life upside down eight years ago, the man who had shown her with his easily given, extraordinary devotion how incapable of loving she was.

Was she a fool for asking him to stay and help?

Maybe she just wanted him around to handle the nuclear waste. Yes, that was the reason, and was, actually, a darn good one. Avoiding that job alone was worth any amount of emotional torture, although she mentally vowed not to let herself *feel* any emotional pain.

She'd been there and done that—with terrible results. Lesson learned. She'd make sure Aiden didn't get to her again.

She followed the delicious smell in the air to the kitchen, her stomach rumbling, looking forward to one of his fluffy omelettes. If she remembered right, he could whip up a great omelette in record time. She'd practically lived off of them when they'd been dating. His cooking for her had always made her feel well cared for.

As she neared the kitchen, she heard him humming a song off-key. She stopped in the doorway and watched him for a moment, her heartbeat accelerating. He stood at the stove, tending the frying pan, a blue dish towel flung over his shoulder. He deftly flipped the omelette like a pro, then moved to the sink and began to rinse off the cutting board he'd used. What was it about a man who knew his way around a kitchen? Why did she find that so darned attractive? Was it because that was something she'd never, ever seen her father do? Or maybe because it took an extraordinary man to feel comfortable in a kitchen?

Or maybe because the only times she'd ever seen

Aiden in the kitchen, he'd been cooking for her because he cared about her?

She fidgeted, shaking her head. Didn't matter. She had to quit thinking about Aiden as anything but someone who could help her deal with Laura. Period. She simply needed to pretend nothing was wrong and everything would be just fine.

Aiden turned and snagged her gaze with his. "Hey, there you are." He raised the spatula in greeting. "You managed to get her into the playpen without her waking up?"

"Do you hear any crying?" She moved into the kitchen, unable to resist smiling smugly.

He cocked his head to the side, listening. "Ah. Blessed silence."

"No small feat." She went over to the stove and eyed the omelette cooking in the frying pan, took a big whiff, noting on her way by that Aiden had cleaned up Laura's cereal mess and had already set a place at the table, complete with orange juice and buttered toast. Colleen's mouth watered. "And blessed food, too."

He chuckled under his breath. "You must be starving."

"Ravenous. I haven't had one spare minute to eat all morning."

"Well, sit down," he said, pulling her chair out with a flourish, "and I'll bring you your breakfast."

A bemused smile on her face, she sat. "You don't have to wait on me, you know." She picked up the toast and nibbled on the corner.

He flicked off the stove and picked up the frying pan. "Ah, but I do. Anyone who could get that baby to stop crying and go to sleep deserves to be rewarded." He scooped up the large omelette with the spatula and placed the fragrant egg concoction on her plate. "Eat up—oh, wait, I forgot something." He stepped to the refrigerator and opened it. After a few seconds of searching, he pulled a ketchup bottle out and presented it to her. "I know you'll want this."

She pulled in her chin, set the toast down and took the ketchup from him. "You remember I like ketchup on my omelettes?"

He looked at her. All at once, she felt as if she were drowning in his emerald gaze. "I remember a lot of things about you," he said in a soft, deep voice.

He abruptly turned away, and she could have sworn he mumbled, "Maybe too much." She imagined Aiden didn't have many positive memories of their relationship, which, while physically satisfying, had been strewn with emotional land mines that always blew up.

That explosiveness had manifested itself in verbal battles, when he'd tried to get her to open up to him and she hadn't been able to allow herself to. She'd always been so conscious of keeping herself emotionally separate from him for fear that if he found out too much about her, he'd discover her deepest, most shameful secret—how flawed and incapable of loving she was.

In the end, she'd chosen to simply leave rather than stay and fight so darn hard to keep her secret. It would have been heartbreaking to have had to stay and face his inevitable scorn when he found out she lacked the most basic of human capabilities.

Then, he would have walked away, just as her parents had, and that was something she never could have dealt with.

Dragging her thoughts away from their rocky past, she watched him putter around the kitchen, cleaning up. She couldn't help but notice his broad, capable shoulders, how thoroughly masculine he looked, even while performing routine domestic tasks with a dish towel over his shoulder.

She squirmed on the hard chair and pressed a hand to her knot-filled stomach.

Her stomach growled in protest, reminding her that she needed to eat, even if Aiden's presence bothered her enough to chase her appetite clear to China.

She set her jaw and grabbed the ketchup, opened the lid and squirted a ton of it onto her eggs. She dug into the omelette, discovering when she did so that it was plain cheese—her favorite. Again, she was surprised that he'd remembered what she liked—although when she thought about it, she'd done the shopping and knew that cheese had been the only filling ingredient in the fridge.

She was sure Aiden wasn't thinking in terms of what she did or didn't like anymore.

She ate, savoring the flavors and warm, gooey cheese, relaxing gradually as the food filled her empty stomach. Maybe her tension and off-whack mood were simply caused by hunger.

Aiden finished loading the dishwasher and turned around and leaned back against the counter. He crossed one ankle over the other and folded his arms over his wide chest. "So, how is it?" He nodded to her half-eaten omelette.

"Really good," she said, determined not to pay any attention to how he filled the small kitchen with his large body. "Thank you."

He inclined his head. "You're welcome. I remembered that cheese was your favorite. Lucky I found what I needed for that."

She choked, then managed to swallow the hunk of egg stuck in her throat. "You remembered that, too?"

He gave her a vaguely irritated look. "Of course I remembered. I must have made a thousand of these."

Her stomach twisted at the reminder of all of the wonderful things he used to do for her. She smiled brightly to cover up her discomfort, and held her egg-laden fork in the air, then brought it to her mouth and pulled off the piece of ketchup-covered omelette with her mouth. She chewed and swallowed. "A thousand and one now. Thank you again for making this." She took a sip of juice, looking at him over the rim of the glass.

He smiled and bent down, bringing his body and scent so close she could barely think, let alone breathe. "You're welcome." His gaze dropped to her mouth. In an instant, like an electric current, tension arced through the air, changing the atmosphere in the room from light and teasing to dark and erotic. Her heart thumped in her chest in a way that it hadn't since those days in another life, days spent with Aiden, pressed close to his heart, his voice whispering how much he loved her in the dark.

Before she knew what was happening, he'd closed the distance between them, putting his lips on hers.

Heat exploded inside her, and she didn't, *couldn't,* pull away. Mercy, she couldn't even put together a coherent thought with his mouth on hers, his big, masculine body so close she could smell him, taste him, want him. Kissing him it was easy to imagine that his strong, capable arms would shelter her from all her bad memories of being unwanted and unloved.

She melted into him, needing to be cocooned in his warm body. His large hand moved to the back of her head and held her steady while his mouth pried hers open. His tongue caressed hers, a stroke of pure fire, and her blood turned hot and molten. Oh, how she wanted to stand up and lead him down to her bed and make love all day long.

A baby's cry echoed through her hazy brain. She ignored it, concentrating instead on kissing Aiden to within an inch of his life. When his hands trailed down her back to pull her to her feet, then drew her closer, so close she could feel his—

Baby crying!

She jerked away and stumbled back. "Laura!" she panted, briefly noting the confused, sort of astonished expression on Aiden's face. "Laura's crying." She clumsily turned on her heel and left the kitchen.

She hurried into Maggie's room on shaking legs, one thought reverberating in her mind.

What have I done?

Her stomach a mass of nerves, she set aside that question temporarily to take care of Laura. She cooed nonsense words to her, which Colleen vaguely wondered how she knew, and awkwardly picked her up from amidst the fuzzy blankets in the playpen. The baby settled down right away, and began drifting off to sleep again.

Colleen slowly went back out, her cheeks burning, Laura in her arms, mouthing "She's okay" to Aiden, who hovered in the kitchen doorway, a concerned, inquisitive look taking the place of his dazed expression of moments before.

Colleen sank onto the couch and Laura shifted in her arms, snuggling closer. Gazing down at the sleeping baby, she roamed her eyes over Laura's soft-looking skin, long, dark eyelashes, and cupid's-bow mouth. Without warning, Colleen's chest tightened and a foreign tenderness seeped through her.

She looked up, unable to help smiling at the new feeling, and saw Aiden standing across the small living room, as still as stone, gazing intently at her, his eyes alight with…tenderness? Admiration?

Uneasy with his scrutiny, she looked at Laura again, who shifted in her sleep, whimpered, and then shoved her thumb into her mouth. Colleen smiled again, and her curiosity about Aiden got the better of her. Taking a deep breath, she looked back up. But all she saw was his back as he whipped around and hurried into the kitchen, like the hounds of hell were nipping at his heels.

She frowned. Had she imagined that warm look in his eyes? She sat, her mind spinning for a few minutes, wondering why she cared what he thought of her and, of course, what in the name of heaven had come over her when she'd responded to his kiss instead of pulling away as she should have.

Maybe her long, sleepless night had damaged her ability to make rational decisions.

Thank goodness Laura had awakened, crying, and stopped the kiss before it went any further. There was nothing like the shrill, eardrum-breaking screams of a fussy baby to bring reality crashing down on a person.

A cold, hard reality that slapped Colleen upside the head and harshly reminded her that she had no business letting Aiden so close again. No business kissing him. No business losing control, which would only open her up to being vulnerable.

So what did that mean?

The answer was amazingly simple. She would just have to be darn sure she didn't have another brain freeze and kiss Aiden again.

No matter how much she longed for the feel of his lips on hers and his strong arms around her.

She wouldn't forget that, no matter what.

Mindful of the sleeping baby in the next room, Aiden squatted and put the frying pan into the cupboard, wishing he could fling the cupboard door closed. He quietly closed it, then stood, shaking his head.

Why was he letting the memory of Colleen rocking

Laura to sleep burn itself into his brain to twist his insides around like a pretzel? To foolishly make him believe that she was different from the inwardly focused woman who'd cut out his heart?

He didn't want to let himself think about Colleen in any terms but business. After the wrenching horrors he'd seen and the guilt he lived with, she wasn't the unchallenging, uncomplicated kind of woman he wanted, not to mention his lingering bitterness over how she'd ruthlessly ended their relationship the last time. How could he ever forget that?

Despite his best intentions, being with Colleen was getting more complicated by the minute, especially with Laura involved. Strangely, all he seemed to be able to do was be impressed, and warmed to the core, by how she was handling the baby.

And that hot kiss…

Get real. That kiss had been a mistake, period. He'd been sucked into his attraction and had acted on his male instincts instead of reminding himself of all the reasons he could never get involved with Colleen again. He'd loved her once and had been kicked in the teeth in return, spurring him to run overseas to a place full of suffering, a place that continued to haunt him. No damn way he was going to repeat that costly mistake.

He grabbed a sponge and wiped the counter. Satisfied he had his head back on straight, he rinsed out the sponge and put it on the drain board. He headed back out to the living room, confident he could deal with Colleen now that he'd looked at things from the right angle, kind of like the perfect camera shot.

The room was empty and he figured she was trying to put Laura back to sleep in her playpen. He lowered himself onto the couch just as Colleen walked from the hall into the living room, looking stressed out, her arms thankfully baby-less.

She stopped next to the couch and raised her arms in the air, stretching. Her T-shirt rode up and exposed a strip of her firm-looking stomach. "How do people do this for eighteen years?"

Unable to help himself, his gaze remained stuck on that tantalizing patch of skin. "Uh, well…you mean… stretch?"

She waved a hand in front of his face. "Of course not. I mean, how do people take care of kids for that long?" She dropped down onto the far end of the couch, shaking her head.

He swiped a hand over his face. "Oh. Yeah. That."

"Are you okay?" she asked, leaning closer.

Her peachy scent wafted over him, all light and feminine, and warmth bloomed south of the border. "Sure, sure." He shifted on the couch, wishing his damn body was as smart as his head. Then again, he could handle lust, right? Lust didn't hurt. Didn't squeeze his heart till it bled. Didn't send a man half-way across the world to witness babies dying, to plant seeds of guilt that could never be overcome.

Colleen drew her legs up underneath her, twisted to face him and put her elbow up on the back of the couch. "Listen, uh…about that kiss…" Her face colored becomingly.

"Yeah, I've been thinking about it, too." He adjusted his body so he was looking right at her and could, in typical male fashion, harmlessly enjoy the view while it lasted. "It was a mistake. I'm sorry."

She nodded, not meeting his gaze. "I know."

"We always did have chemistry, didn't we?" They'd spent a lot of time in bed, he realized now, rather than really talking.

"Yes, we did. But giving in to that now, as you said, would be wrong," she observed, the realist in her surging forth, reminding her why she and Aiden didn't have a chance in hell of not only overcoming their history, but of making their way past her flaw to everlasting happiness.

Aiden leaned back on the couch and looked at the ceiling. He then cast his sea-green gaze her way. "You've always felt that way, haven't you?" A spark of bitterness flashed in his eyes. "Getting involved has always been a big fat mistake, right? Why is that?"

Oh, mercy, she didn't want to have this conversation, had *never* wanted to have it. But what, really, was the harm now? Eight years ago she hadn't been able to face the shame of her past and its harsh ramifications on their relationship. Rather than opening up, afraid of his reaction, she'd left.

Now they'd both gone on with their lives, and even though they'd been thrown together for "The Baby

Chronicles'' that was as far as their relationship went, as far as she could ever let it go.

They didn't mean anything to each other anymore. His opinion of her didn't matter. Did it?

She bit her lip, surprised at the vague sting of tears pressing at the back of her eyelids and astonished that Aiden still had the ability to bring forth such vulnerability and emotion in her.

She sniffed, willing her pesky tears away, and gathered her courage to dump the story out and clear the air. But before she could respond, Aiden touched her arm. "After all these years, I still wonder why you walked away from me." He smiled uneasily. "I mean, I always sensed that romantic comedies were horror films for you, but I never really knew why."

She smiled without humor and picked at a nub on the couch. "I've never told you about my childhood, have I?" She'd kept the reality of her foster-care years from him, and everybody else, too, feeling so very ashamed her parents hadn't loved her enough to want to keep her.

He drew his eyebrows together. "Right. All I know is that you aren't close to your parents, you have no brothers or sisters, and that you grew up in Beaverton, but that's it."

She abruptly stood and began to pace in front of the couch. "There's not much to tell. My parents weren't into parenting. They neglected me, leaving me alone all the time." She paused to tamp down the familiar, hated ache. "The truth is, they dumped me in foster care when I was nine. I haven't heard from them since. I was shuffled through several foster-care homes, and finally ended up with an alcoholic woman who verbally abused me and forced me to be a live-in baby-sitter for the younger kids.''

"Oh, Colleen, I'm sorry. I had no idea,'' he said, his eyes soft and sympathetic.

"The worst part was, I couldn't help but think that my parents' abandonment was my fault.'' Moisture crested in her eyes and rolled down her cheeks.

Aiden rose and stepped close, his face reflecting distress, but she waved him off. "No,'' she managed to say. "Let me finish. I've always known that there was something wrong with me, some…flaw inside that made my parents not love me.'' She looked at him, shaking her head. "So, you see, it wasn't you, it was me. That defect is still there, and it will never go away. I've never been able to nurture any kind of relationship. I just don't know how to do that.''

"So that's why you left?''

She nodded and looked at the floor, swiping at the tears on her cheeks, unable to bear to look at him and see the scorn in his eyes.

"Why didn't you tell me this then?''

She wrapped her arms around her waist, feeling chilled and achy. "I was…ashamed.'' Her voice broke and more tears welled in her eyes and tumbled down her face.

Instantly, Aiden was there, wrapping her in his arms from behind. He pressed his mouth to her ear. "I wish you'd told me. We could have worked it out.''

"No. There's no way to fix what isn't there."

He grasped her shoulders and turned her around to face him. Green fire burned in his eyes. "Your parents not loving you was not your fault. It was their fault, Colleen, not yours."

She stared at him, shaking her head. "But if I'd been different—"

"No! Don't even say it. Your stupid parents should have been different, not you. You were an innocent child, for heaven's sake. They let you down, Colleen, not the other way around."

She'd been over this a hundred, maybe a thousand times, and even though on the surface Aiden's opinion seemed valid, it wasn't. She was flawed. Unlovable. Unable to love. Her parents had proved it by deserting her, and her failed relationship with Aiden had proved it. She hadn't known how to love the most wonderful man on the planet, had actually been able to walk away from him when he'd offered her everything. Any whole woman would have grabbed on to him and never let him go. That alone proved her theory.

She gave him a wobbly smile. "I appreciate what you're saying, but I don't agree."

He stared at her, moving his head slowly from side to side. "You are a wonderful fool, Colleen." He gently shook her shoulders and bent closer. "You've taken on responsibility for your parents' crummy behavior, and let that ruin your life—our life, or the one we could have had together."

Fresh tears brimmed in her eyes when she thought

about what she'd had to walk away from, what she'd lost. "Do you think I don't know that? Do you think I don't know what I gave up when I left you?" she whispered, her voice breaking. "Believe me, that's always been like a stone in my heart, Aiden. But that's just the way things had to be."

She pulled from his grasp and turned her back on him and his comfort and understanding, the cold, hard truth of the present situation bearing down on her, knocking some sense into her.

She was still the flawed person her parents had abandoned.

She turned to him, ignoring the soft concern in his eyes, and said, "Nothing's changed. That's the way things had to be then, and that's the way they have to be now."

She walked into the kitchen and her heart shattered into millions of tiny, jagged pieces inside her chest, cutting her from the inside out. She embraced the slicing pain, letting it drive home unvarnished reality.

She was a fool for letting herself be sucked into Aiden's heartwarming appeal again, a fool for believing on some blind level that she would ever be able to rise above the truth of what she lacked—the ability to love him.

She saw now that she'd been hoping that she was different. But she had to accept the truth: she was as incomplete as she'd ever been.

Chapter Six

Aiden wasn't that surprised when Colleen had looked at him with tears in her big blue eyes and then left him standing alone in the living room. He understood her better now, and could see around his own bitterness long enough to comprehend why she'd run from him before.

For an instant, he wanted to call her back, take her in his arms and wipe away her pain. But that impulse died quickly. Even though the reality of her loveless, neglected, lonely childhood made him ache with sadness and made her desertion easier to understand, he still couldn't allow himself to want her again.

Realistically, a relationship with Colleen would be a mistake. She was a test he didn't want to face, a challenge he'd failed once before. If anything, now that he knew why she'd dumped him, he had even more reason to keep his distance. She had some pretty heavy-duty baggage—so did he—and a relationship would never survive their problems.

So he told Colleen he needed to check his gear and left her in the kitchen chopping vegetables, promising to return later for the baby-bathing lesson. He returned to his condo, ate some potato chips for an early lunch and occupied his mind by rechecking his already organized photography gear, making sure he'd be ready to roll as soon as the weather cleared.

Colleen called him when Laura woke up an hour later. He went back to Colleen's condo and gave her a quick baby-bathing lesson, a task that created an unexpected ache in his chest a mile wide he refused to dissect. Determined to keep the necessary emotional and physical distance from Colleen, he then went to check on the weather, which had looked on the verge of clearing when he'd walked to Colleen's unit.

Luckily, the weather *had* cleared, leaving a few scattered clouds that cut the glare of the sun and softened the light enough, in Aiden's opinion, to go ahead and take pictures of babies.

He rounded up the parents and their kids, anxious to get started, anticipating taking cute pictures of chubby-cheeked, happy babies.

Dream on.

From the moment he touched his camera, the shoot went wrong. None of the babies were interested in doing anything but crying, screaming or whimpering whenever he was around, creating a kind of baby chaos he wasn't prepared for.

But he had a job to do, a job that could launch his career as a baby photographer, so he doggedly pushed forward, determined to make the shoot a success.

He settled on a grassy area shaded by juniper trees and surrounded by wildflowers for the setting. He did his best to remain patient in the middle of bedlam, using every photographer's trick to get the babies' attention long enough to click off a few shots. He smiled. He cooed. He made silly sounds. He rattled toys, waved stuffed animals in the air and made funny faces. Anything to get their attention.

But he didn't seem to have the knack. Just when he was freaking out and felt his plans for the future as a baby photographer about to be ruined by five screaming baby conspirators, Colleen passed the equipment she was helping him with to a parent and jumped in to help.

To his admiration and relief, she remained calm and good-natured in the midst of five very cranky, uncooperative infants. She comforted, patted and held the babies, and generally ran around and made herself indispensable during the shoot. She managed to calm every one down just long enough to get a good picture.

Finally, after two hours of on-again, off-again coddling, cajoling and teamwork, all the kids went into meltdown mode and he grudgingly admitted to a frazzled-looking Colleen that he had enough material to work with.

The relieved parents scooped up their children and headed back to their condos, most likely to keel over alongside their exhausted, cranky infants.

Colleen wearily picked up a fussy, red-faced Laura, hooked the diaper bag over her shoulder and looked over at him, her bone-deep weariness evident in her eyes. "I know this is a lot to ask, but could you help me out for a while tonight? The thought of taking care of this little gal on my own literally exhausts me."

Aiden had hoped to head back to his own place and enjoy the blessed silence, and if he had any brains, he should avoid being with Colleen. "Are you sure that's a good idea?"

She inclined her head. "Hey, I know where you're coming from. I've told myself I need to steer clear of you, too."

He raised his eyebrows, surprised by her honesty. Before he could say anything, she lifted a hand in the air, stopping him. "I'm not going to beat around the proverbial bush about this, Aiden. We both know that after that kiss, we should keep some distance. But frankly, I'm worn out and genuinely doubt my ability to take care of Laura. Given that, I'm willing to put up with you if you agree to put up with me." She gave him a mock-stern look. "But no more kissing, right? At least not for a day or two."

He liked her forthrightness, and he had to admit, seeing her standing there, her golden hair falling out of her ponytail, her cheeks pink, a cranky baby in her arms, did a major number on his resistance. Besides, he owed her. Big-time. The shoot, he suspected, would have been doomed without her patience, calm and cheerful demeanor.

How would he ever do this job on his own?

Determined not to dwell on that depressing question now, he zipped up a camera bag. "Sounds like a deal. I need to haul my gear back and take a shower. How about if I meet you at your place at…" He glanced at his watch. "Five-thirty?"

She smiled, a look of pure relief spreading across her flushed face. "That sounds great." She turned to leave, then looked over her shoulder. "I'm going to give her a snack, and then maybe another bath since she looks sweaty, then call the hospital to check on Maggie. I'll see you then."

He watched Colleen walk away, Laura now propped on her hip. She bent her head down and said something in Laura's ear, then pulled back and smiled at her. Laura chortled and waved her arms in the air.

Aiden smiled, shaking his head. Again, he couldn't help noticing how the two of them looked so natural together. Colleen might think she needed help with Laura, but she'd been a genuine nurturer today. She'd handled the babies with a surprising amount of poise, confidence and patience.

Very unlike the woman he'd known in another life. So much more centered and selfless.

He drew his warm thoughts up short. Big deal. He'd learned his lesson. No way was he going to make the same mistake he'd made by falling in love with her eight years ago, only to have his heart bombed out.

This time, he knew what a mistake getting involved with Colleen would be. He had his eyes wide open.

He'd just have to be damn sure he kept them that way.

Later that evening, after Colleen put an exhausted Laura to sleep and she and Aiden washed and dried the dinner dishes, both of them fell onto the couch.

Aiden was worn-out.

Colleen wearily pushed her hair away from her face and looked at him from where she'd sprawled on the other end of the couch. "I haven't worked this hard since…well, since never."

Aiden stretched him arms in the air, then leaned back, relaxing. "You did work your tail off today. I couldn't have done the shoot without you. Thanks."

"Those babies were a handful, weren't they?"

He nodded. "I had no idea taking pictures of little kids would be so much work." A small dart of apprehension shot through him. Was he really cut out to photograph unpredictable babies?

Her gaze turned puzzled. "So why do you want to be a baby photographer? Why not stick with something easier?"

Wariness joined the apprehension inside him. Colleen's questions would undoubtedly lead to more, and he sure wasn't up for talking about his past or the reasons he wanted to become a baby photographer. "I like kids, I like to take pictures," he said, shrugging casually, not meeting her eyes. "Seemed like a logical choice."

"Actually, it doesn't to me." She tucked her feet underneath herself. "It seems odd that you gave up a lucrative career as an internationally acclaimed photojournalist for something as domestic as taking pictures of babies."

He remained silent, hoping she would drop her current train of thought. Despite how well he and Colleen had worked together all day and how comfortable their evening had become, opening up about his reasons for ending his career overseas was out of the question. It would be too revealing and painful to discuss his emotional scars.

Hell, he could barely think about the things that haunted him, the guilt that ate at him every day, much less actually verbalize them.

When he didn't answer her, she leaned in, bringing the scent of fresh peaches with her. "So why are you home, Aiden? Why *did* you give up your career?"

He shifted on the couch, away from her tempting scent. "No real reason," he lied. "I guess I needed a change of scenery." Which was true. A man could only live like a nomad, traveling from one war-torn country to another, for so long.

"Oh, come on," she said, her voice cajoling. She leaned nearer still, her arm on the couch in back of him. "I see the new lines in your face. What happened?"

Terrible, horrific things I couldn't stop.

He closed his eyes briefly, willing away the visions

that had burned themselves onto his brain like a white-hot branding iron, pictures of bombed-out villages and homeless, starving families.

He pulled in a deep, calming breath and looked at Colleen, attempting a casual smile. "I guess I've aged."

She frowned, creating appealing little creases between her eyebrows. "And...?"

"And what?"

"And, surely there's more than just that. I see more than simple aging in your face." Her voice was soft, gentle. Sensitive. She settled back and stared at him, her head cocked to the side, glimpses of understanding evident in her gaze. "I see...shadows."

He raised his eyebrows, surprised by her perceptiveness and sensitivity, things that had been in short supply in her eight years ago.

She actually saw the differences in him.

He *did* have shadows inside him, huge, dark ones that wouldn't let him rest or forget the atrocities he'd seen. What he'd experienced had left its mark in a profound way that obviously showed.

Damn. He didn't want anybody to know how deeply he'd been affected by the last eight years, how much guilt he carried around.

How he'd failed all of those children.

He turned and looked at her again. She stared at him, her gorgeous blue eyes soft with a kind of compassion and understanding he'd never seen in her before.

An ache formed inside, radiating outward, and for

just a moment he wanted to dump out what he'd been through. He wished he could share with her the terrible things he'd seen, things that had cut into him, burned him from the inside out.

But he couldn't.

He didn't want her pity, and he couldn't bring the horror to the surface to scald him all over again. He wanted to bury all of it, obliterate it with a new job, a new life, a fresh start.

Colleen didn't need to know what haunted his dreams, what had branded itself deep in his soul, changing him forever.

So he ignored the ache, shoving it down into its cage, and said, "You're imagining things, Colleen. I changed careers because I was tired of living away from my family and tired of living out of a suitcase. End of story." He stood and rubbed his hands together, intent on changing the subject. "So, what's for dessert?"

She didn't respond for a few long seconds. She simply sat on the couch, staring at him, unblinking. Then she shook her head, her mouth pressed into a line, unfolded her legs from underneath her and stood, her thumbs hooked on the front pockets of her shorts. "Fine. Avoid my questions. I understand why you wouldn't want to share anything like that with me. I never was a very good listener, was I?" She put herself into motion and walked by him. "I'll go round up some ice cream."

He reached out to snag her elbow and stop her, but he let his hand fall away at the last moment.

Let her go. Don't ask for trouble.

He watched her walk away, then swiped a hand over his face. He hated her thinking that he didn't want to share his scars with her because of *her*. Surprisingly, she, of all people, would understand his pain because of her lonely, neglected childhood and the ache she'd lived with for most of her life.

No, she wasn't the problem. He couldn't reveal the unspeakable horrors etched on his brain because of what lived inside *him*.

His guilt. His haunting memories. His private demons.

And nobody could help him with any of those heartbreaking things—especially not Colleen.

To lend weight to the conviction, he couldn't possibly forget that Colleen was a challenge he had failed once—miserably.

He could never forget that after the hell he'd lived through, he didn't have it in him to fail again.

Later that night, long after midnight, Colleen lay in bed, wide awake despite her totally exhausting day.

To her irritation, she couldn't get Aiden out of her mind. All she could think about was how patient and calm he'd been with the fussy babies during the shoot today. The guy had bent over backward to find creative ways to get the little ones to cooperate, and hadn't once lost his cool. He'd merely smiled that gorgeous smile and gamely looked for another silly way to make them smile.

He'd also gone out of his way to help her with

Laura all day, which, really, had gone above and beyond the call of duty, especially because Laura hadn't really ever warmed up to him.

Especially since they both knew they should be keeping their distance.

It wasn't hard for Colleen to see why she'd been so drawn to him eight years ago. He was a caring, wonderful man.

That thought was enough to create a nice little boulder of tension inside her.

She flung the blankets off her too-warm, tense body and hummed ''Rudolph the Red-Nosed Reindeer'' to distract herself, a song she'd always sung to herself when she was little to drown out the sound of her parents' fights.

Inevitably, however, once she'd sung five verses and cooled her body down, Aiden crept back into her mind, and she homed in on the one-sided conversation they'd had earlier. After being so touched and impressed by the man she'd seen at the shoot, she hadn't been able to stop herself from asking him some very pointed questions about why he'd left his career behind, about the subtle differences she'd noted in him.

He hadn't opened up to her, though, and surprisingly, his stubborn unwillingness to talk, his shutting her out, had stung. She'd opened up to him and told him about her less-than-wonderful childhood. Why couldn't he do the same?

She rolled over in bed and flung an arm over her face, willing all thoughts of one Aiden Forbes from her mind. She was determined to ignore his *knock, knock, knock* on the door to her heart. She'd almost answered the knock before and had come too close to letting him barge through.

This time the door would stay firmly closed.

She would pick up Maggie, who was due to be discharged from the hospital tomorrow, and return to Portland with her and Laura. Colleen would complete ''The Baby Chronicles'' and she and Aiden would never have any reason to see each other again. Her life would return to its normal routine, and that would be that.

She closed her eyes and willed sleep to come, trying to ignore the familiar emptiness eating away inside and the dull, persistent ache that moved through her when she thought about spending the rest of her life alone.

But it didn't work.

Darn if she didn't wish in a tiny corner of her brain that she could chop the door down with an ax and just let him in.

Good thing she had more sense than that.

Chapter Seven

Colleen sat at her desk, her laptop open, her notes in full view, staring into space when she should be working on "The Baby Chronicles."

Three days had passed since she'd picked Maggie up at the hospital in Bend and returned to Portland. Thank heaven she was recuperating nicely after her appendectomy. Her mother had come to town to help with Laura while Maggie recovered.

The news wasn't as good concerning Aiden. Even though Colleen hadn't seen him since they'd parted ways in Sun Mountain on Monday, she still hadn't been able to shake him from her thoughts.

She only hoped that eventually, after she hadn't admired his gorgeous smile, breathed in his sexy, unique scent, and watched him calmly handle babies who screamed when he was around, she'd be able to banish him from her brain for good. Their kiss, especially, had been on her mind.

Yes, she'd made a monumentally stupid error by kissing him at Sun Mountain. She heartily acknowledged that, fully owning her own dumb blunder. Now it was time to get smart, move past her mistakes and get on with her life.

Thank heaven "The Baby Chronicles" was almost complete, which would wipe away any possible reason to see him again. She knew from a parting conversation with Aiden at Sun Mountain that he was going to examine the photos he'd taken over the weekend, which he was planning to spend at his parents' house in Oak Valley, a small town about an hour south of Portland.

Any reason to see him was now almost nonexistent. All she needed was time to settle back into LAA2—Life After Aiden, Part 2—and forget how much she wished in some obscure, naive corner of her heart that she could take a magic pill and miraculously be gifted with the ability to love him.

But this was real life, not some fluffy fairy tale, and she couldn't. With that reality in mind, she went back to "The Baby Chronicles," hoping work would take her mind off Aiden.

Five minutes later, she heard Joe boom, "Colleen, my office, please."

She rose and made her way to his office. Joe had been out of town since Monday and she was sure that he wanted an update on "The Baby Chronicles,"

which was due to go to press next week, after Aiden
turned in the pictures he wanted to use.

She stopped in the door. "You yelled?"

He gave her the obligatory stern look. "Yeah.
How's 'Baby' coming along?"

"I'm working on the copy now. I'll be done in
plenty of time."

"I haven't been in contact with Aiden. He on
schedule?"

She nodded. "I think so. I know he's planning on
going to his parents' house this weekend to make the
final photo cuts."

Joe's eyes lit up. "He's going to be seeing his
mom?"

"Yeah, I guess," she said, lowering her eyebrows.
"Why?"

Joe stood and began pacing. "When he applied for
this job, he sent some really wonderful black-and-
white photos of babies and kids he took while overseas."

"Okay." She remembered Joe mentioning them
the day she'd encountered Aiden in Joe's office and
learned she'd be working with Aiden.

"He wasn't willing to hand over more photos when
I asked him, but I still want them for 'Baby.' Imagine
them juxtaposed against the pics he took at Sun
Mountain." He rubbed his hands together. "It would
be a poignant contrast—babies, in color, next to
babies in black and white. I think it would give a
whole new dimension to the piece."

"Sounds great." Joe might be a gruff, hard-driving

taskmaster, but he was also an editorial genius. "But what does this have to do with me?"

He pointed at her. "You and Aiden know each other. I want you to go to his parents' house with him and find a way to either convince him to cough up the photos or talk his mom into allowing them to be used in print."

Dread congealed in her stomach. The one thing she didn't want to do was spend any more time with Aiden, stirring up impossible dreams. "Joe, there has to be another way—"

"I don't think so," he said, taking his ancient tweed jacket from the back of his chair. "You're friends, right? Should be no problem convincing either him or his mom to agree to the photos being included." He put his coat on and adjusted his tie.

"Why don't you just ask him for the photos again?" she asked, determined to find another solution, one that didn't involve any contact with Aiden.

"I did, and he blew me off, so time for plan B. Sometimes you have to go after things in a creative, unexpected way." He patted her shoulder. "I have a gut feeling you'll be able to convince him."

Aiden, she was sure, wouldn't want to be doing her any favors. "How am I going to invite myself along?" she asked, near panic.

He shrugged, moving toward the door. "You two are colleagues as well as friends. I'm sure you'll come up with something. Listen, I gotta run, I'm late. Don't fail me now, Colleen." He exited his office, leaving Colleen standing there alone, terror-filled anxiety running rampant at the disturbing thought of allowing Aiden the chance to get under her skin again.

She woodenly walked back to her desk, shaking her head. So much for avoiding Aiden. Her boss had just demanded she accompany him for another weekend away. From a personal standpoint, not a good move.

The last thing she should do was spend time with either Aiden or his large, loving family. It would only remind her how lacking her own family was and of the pain she'd lived with. Eight years ago, she'd successfully avoided meeting his family for that exact reason.

But her boss had spoken, and unless she wanted to jeopardize her job, she had no choice but to do as Joe asked. From where he stood, it was obviously no big deal for her to make this plan work; he had no idea of her and Aiden's angst-ridden history or of her compelling reasons to stay permanently away from him.

And she had to admit, including the black-and-white overseas photos was a brilliant idea. From a purely practical, job standpoint, having her name attached to what sounded like a moving, thought-provoking piece might be a career booster.

Okay, she had to be realistic. She had to go along with this for several good reasons, despite wanting to forget about Aiden with everything in her. Buck up. Do the job.

Fine. But how in the world was she going to come up with a believable reason to hang out with Aiden?

Her teeth clamped on her lower lip, she looked

down, her gaze snagging on the laptop, open to ''The Baby Chronicles'' document. The answer was obvious. The only feasible way to approach Aiden was through their mutual project. She'd have to convince him that she needed help and hope he bought it.

Darn it all. Fate wouldn't cut her a break. Just when she thought she was free of Aiden, her editor tangled her back up with him.

A bad feeling descended around her. She only hoped she made it through this weekend unscathed.

Aiden sang along with a Garth Brooks song as he navigated Interstate 5 on his way to Oak Valley.

He'd gotten hung up with a prospective client and had left Portland almost two hours later than he'd planned. He'd called Colleen on her cell phone to tell her, and she'd already been on her way. They'd decided that she'd continue and arrive ahead of him since his parents were expecting her. More than likely she was already there, and he was confident his parents would graciously greet her. Any colleague of his would instantly be made to feel at home.

He couldn't quite believe he was going to be spending another weekend with Colleen. Not what he'd expected, or wanted. Deep in his gut he knew that being around her wasn't a brilliant idea. But when she'd called, sounding desperate, wanting his help with the article, his journalistic instincts hadn't let him refuse. For purely selfish reasons he wanted this piece to be as good as it could possibly be. He was willing to be around Colleen if she needed help making that a reality.

He didn't want to sacrifice the time he'd promised to spend with his parents, either, especially the day he'd promised to spend with his dad fishing. There was no reason he and Colleen couldn't work together for a while longer. Look how well they'd done that last night in Sun Mountain. They'd worked side by side, taking care of Laura, with no negative ramifications. Granted, Colleen had pried a bit about his reasons for returning home, but he'd successfully deflected her questions and kept his heart, and secrets about his haunting memories, safe.

This was no big deal, strictly a working weekend, a chance to improve the article. Nothing more threatening than that.

He exited the freeway and turned left, heading in the direction of Oak Valley two miles away, nestled in the Willamette Valley south of Salem, the capitol of Oregon.

It was a beautiful summer afternoon, and he enjoyed the rolling hills, quaint farmhouses and huge, leafy oak trees rising like huge sentinels periodically along the road and across the country landscape.

He always felt so at peace when he returned home, and that feeling had intensified since he'd come back from overseas. How lucky he was to live in a beautiful, unspoiled place like Oregon, a place that hadn't been devastated and torn apart by bombs and war and hate.

He gripped the steering wheel, and through sheer

determination drove on, faster than he should. He was anxious to be in Oak Valley, the quiet, traditional little town where he'd spent his wonderful childhood. Hopefully there he could hold his grueling memories at bay—or better yet, get rid of them altogether.

A few minutes later, he entered Oak Valley, finally able to breathe. A tentative smile formed on his lips. He loved this place, always felt so secure and grounded while here. Oak Valley oozed small-town USA, especially since the town council had carefully maintained the town's charming look by completely remodeling the storefronts on Main Street and several side streets to resemble an old-fashioned boardwalk. Big baskets of flowers hung off every lamppost and rustic benches lined the boardwalk. Colorful windsocks blew in the summer breeze.

As he drove through, he looked at his father's medical office right on the boardwalk in the middle of Main Street, the words Mr. Commitment stenciled in gold letters on the window below Brady Forbes, M.D.

Aiden smiled at his father's nickname, which had been bestowed upon him several years ago when the people of Oak Valley had discovered that Doc Forbes was as good at helping them heal their romantic relationships as he was at helping them heal their bodies. A whole side business had emerged, although his dad dispensed his relationship advice for free.

His father always took Friday afternoons off, so Aiden drove on. In all likelihood, his dad would be at home enjoying a glass of lemonade on the porch, as he usually did on nice summer days. If, of course, he'd completed the running list of honey-do chores Aiden's mom kept posted on the refrigerator.

Aiden kept driving down Main Street to Marigold Lane and made a right turn. Five blocks down he turned his SUV into the gravel driveway that led to his parents' turn-of-the-century Victorian house.

The house was set back from the road on a two-acre lot studded by mammoth oak trees. His mom, the chief gardener in the family, had carefully researched plants indigenous to Oregon and had planted them all around to create a natural, unlandscaped look. Closer to the house, rhododendrons, camellias and azaleas bloomed, along with a multitude of colorful, hearty perennials his mom loved.

A tire swing hung suspended from one of the oak trees as it had since he was a boy. How many hours had he and his siblings spent swinging on that old thing; carefree hours he would never experience again?

A sadness for the loss of those untroubled times filled him. How he wished he could turn back the clock and relive those happy-go-lucky days and forget about the things that haunted him.

Shaking himself out of his melancholy haze, forcing himself to ignore his scalding overseas recollections, he turned his attention to the house.

The two-story structure, built in 1901, was painted a calming blue with white trim. A bay window bulged from the left side of the house, and an arched window over the front door added interest. The house also boasted a huge, covered front porch, which was lined

in a white railing and sported a porch swing at one
end and a wrought-iron table and chairs at the other.
At the moment, a group of people clustered around
the table.

He noted Colleen's vehicle, a small, red sports car,
parked near the detached garage, which at one time
had served as a carriage house and had been con-
verted to an apartment. She'd arrived ahead of him,
as he'd expected.

He looked at the table on the porch and zeroed in
on Colleen's bright, curly blond hair right away. His
heart jumped and warmth spread through him. Damn.
He was unaccountably happy to see her, considering
this was nothing more than a working weekend.

He also saw his father, mother, younger brother,
Connor, and, surprisingly, his sister, Jenny, whom he
hadn't expected to see at all since his mom had told
him she was going away to the beach for the weekend. Noticeably absent were his two other siblings,
Kelly, his youngest sister and baby of the family, who
was completing her senior year at the University of
Oregon, and Bryan, the second youngest, who lived
a raucous bachelor life in California.

Aiden got out of his SUV and headed toward the
knot of people on the porch, who had all turned and
were staring at him, expectant looks on their faces.
He took the two wooden stairs up to the porch and
walked toward everybody.

His father stood, the battered red baseball cap he
always wore when he worked in the yard shoved

down over his gray hair, and hailed him. "The happy wanderer arrives."

Aiden met his father's green gaze and smiled, giving him a bear hug. He loved seeing his parents on a regular basis. Thank God he'd come home before old age crept up on them. He and his folks could still enjoy some time together. Aiden planned on routinely going fishing with his dad and antique hunting with his mom as soon as he had himself settled in his rental house in Portland.

He greeted his brother with a handshake. "Hey, Connor. Taking a little time off from the E.R.?"

Connor nodded, a shadow lingering in his hazel eyes. "Actually, I've quit the E.R. I'm moving back to Oak Valley."

Aiden inclined his head, trying to hide his surprise. Connor had always seemed to love being an E.R. doc in Seattle, had seemed to thrive on the long hours and stress.

His father interjected, "Since I'm retiring soon, Connor's come home to take over my practice."

Connor's jaw flexed and he ran a hand through his too-long brown hair, but he said nothing.

Okay. So his dad and Connor were still having problems. He looked at Connor. "If you want to talk, you know where to find me."

"Right," Connor said in his usual as-few-words-as-possible way. Relationships, or anything not explained by science, had never been his brother's forte.

Aiden moved toward the female threesome seated at the table, his apprehension rising a bit when he saw the troubled look in Colleen's eyes. He bent down and kissed his mom on the cheek, noting that she looked as youthful as ever despite the streaks of gray in her short, auburn hair.

He smiled at Jenny, the only blonde among the Forbes clan, then gently kissed her cheek, too, and gave her a gentle squeeze on the arm. Jenny's husband had died in a car accident almost a year ago, while she'd been pregnant with their first child, and it had taken her a long time to join the living again. It was good to see her out and about and see the sparkle in her green eyes, so like his own. "I thought you were going to the beach."

Jenny nodded. "I was. But Martha came down with the flu and canceled."

He nodded, noting that Jenny's daughter, who was usually making toddler trouble, wasn't around. "Where's my darling niece?"

Jenny gestured toward the house. "Inside napping."

Aiden nodded, then turned his full attention to Colleen, who looked great in a pair of snug jeans and a yellow and blue striped short-sleeved shirt, her hair pulled partially up onto the top of her head.

"Hey," he said to her, moving closer, just now noticing the tiny black puppy on her lap. "I see you're getting acquainted with one of Molly's babies," he said, smiling. His parent's toy poodle had had babies nine weeks ago, and the puppy Colleen held was the last one left.

He leaned against the porch railing, trying not to

look so happy to see her, trying not to notice how right that puppy looked nestled in her lap. "I guess you've met everyone."

She smiled awkwardly and stood, holding the baby dog close. "Uh, yes I have. Everyone has been so gracious and welcoming." She sidled closer, biting her lip. "Um, could we…talk?" she asked quietly.

"Sure, we can talk," he murmured, wondering why she looked so uncomfortable. Everybody stared at him for a long moment, and then they all spoke at the same time.

His mom rose and pointed toward the house. "You know, I've got to go check the roast."

His dad mumbled, "I'll help," and followed Aiden's mom into the house.

Jenny chimed in with, "I'll just go…help Mom," then scurried off.

Connor, on the other hand, simply stood leaning against the house, smiling, apparently oblivious to the fact that Colleen wanted to have a private conversation.

Aiden caught his eye and jerked his head toward the house, trying to communicate "Leave, bro" without words.

Connor, who was a smart guy—brilliant, in fact—but frequently missed the gist of anything not documented in a medical text, looked perplexed. After a long pause, he nodded, said, "Ah," held up his hands and sauntered into the house, leaving Aiden alone with Colleen and her uncomfortable-looking expression.

"What's up?" he asked, petting the puppy's soft head.

Colleen cleared her throat. "I just wanted to get a few things straight."

"Okay." He crossed his arms over his chest, wondering where this was going.

"I just wanted to make sure you know that this is strictly a working weekend," she said, echoing his exact thoughts. The fact that she had to justify her presence here aroused his interest more than it really should. Had she had the same inner conversation with herself that he'd had driving down here?

Idly admiring her sparkling blue eyes, he wondered if she was still as attracted to him as he unfortunately was to her if she needed to reiterate her reason for being here. Then again, he was probably reading way too much into everything. She undoubtedly had a handle on her attraction, just as he did. "I know that. Why are you telling me this?"

She smiled half-heartedly. "We kissed at Sun Mountain. I just wanted to be sure you didn't think I was trying to…rekindle something, that's all."

The thought of rekindling anything with Colleen— namely, their sexual relationship—filled him with a raging heat he did his best to ignore. What he needed to pay attention to was that he didn't have any business wanting Colleen in any way and he should be glad she felt the same. "Hey, I'm on the same page. The last thing I want is to relive our history."

She pulled in her chin and scowled, creating cute

little creases between her eyebrows. "Hey, why don't you tell me how you really feel?"

He stared at her, trying to make sense of her scowl and her flip comment. "I'm sorry if that sounded cold, but both of us know that we need to keep our distance."

Colleen nodded, agreeing wholeheartedly, wishing he didn't look so yummy in his beige khakis and the red polo shirt that displayed his well-muscled arms so wonderfully. His heavenly, masculine scent reached her nose, teasing her. Oh, how she wanted to snuggle close to him and have him wrap his strong, capable arms—

She cut that rogue thought off, reminding herself that she was here because her editor had forced her to come, not to wish herself back into Aiden's life.

As she'd sat on the porch with Aiden's wonderful family and seen him arrive, for one brief moment she'd wished she was here for more than just business, that he would walk across the porch and kiss her in greeting. Of course, then their kiss in Sun Mountain had screeched into her brain, and before she knew it, she was deep in Stupid Fantasy City.

Thankfully, she'd squashed those thoughts and returned to reality, feeling the need to reiterate to Aiden that she was here strictly for the work's sake. Maybe if she heard the idea out loud enough she'd begin to get the picture, too, instead of having far-fetched dreams of her and Aiden getting back together every time he looked at her.

Colleen adjusted the pup in her arms and wisely

moved away from Aiden so she could think clearly. "No, you're right. The kiss was great—"

"Yeah, it was, wasn't it?" he murmured in a voice that made her want to relive that kiss—and more.

"But it was a mistake," she said, pitilessly reiterating the truth both to him and herself. "I'm not interested in putting myself somewhere—" She cut herself off before she could say more. She didn't want to share with him how difficult it was for her to be around his loving family without letting the pain of her own scarred, loveless childhood overwhelm her.

"Putting yourself where?" he asked, touching her arm.

His touch seeped into her skin, warming her in a way she both loved and hated. She needed to keep herself cold and separate around him, and his searing touches made that impossible. All she could think of was being close to him again, of losing herself in his heated embrace.

What was she doing, letting him get to her all over again? Lifting her chin, she smiled brightly and said, "Nowhere." She waved a dismissive hand in the air. "I was rambling. What's important is that we need to make sure we keep things in perspective, all right? We foolishly let our guards down and kissed and it can't happen again. I just wanted to make sure you knew that." She looked at him for confirmation that he understood the situation. All he did was nod wordlessly, his lips pressed into a tight line. "Good," she said. "I told your mom I'd help her with dinner, so I'll just go in now."

With the puppy in her arms, she marched into the house, clenching her jaw, angry with herself.

Idiot alert. She'd only been here an hour, and already she was slipping up, not only on the verge of telling Aiden how being around his family made her ache, but also by letting herself yearn for things she could never have. She was here for her job, period.

There would be no more sizzling kisses, no more ridiculous fantasies, no more yearning for something neither of them wanted.

She mentally latched the lock on her heart, threw away the key and vowed she would never look for it again.

After Colleen stomped inside, the puppy clutched to her chest like a shield, Aiden took a walk to clear his head of the unexpected and totally ridiculous regret that had eventually washed over him when Colleen had so eloquently pronounced the reality of their relationship.

Or lack of relationship.

He stared, unseeing, out over his mother's new rose and herb garden, trying to distract himself from how much Colleen's raw practicality ate away at him, wondering why the hell he cared so much. If he had any sense, the truth shouldn't bother him at all, should, in fact, make him jump for joy. He didn't want any kind of personal relationship with her after the hell he'd been through, after she'd burned him so badly before.

He then returned to the house, trying, unsuccessfully, to get Colleen out of his thoughts.

He rubbed a hand over his face, shaking his head. This had to stop.

In the house, after Molly and her pup enthusiastically greeted him, he ran into Connor leaving his dad's study, his face pulled into a frown. Concerned, because nothing ever seemed to faze his brother, Aiden suggested they return to the porch to talk, hoping that listening to Connor's problems would take his mind off his own.

After a little prodding, Connor revealed that he and their dad were having a "mild disagreement"—an understatement, Aiden suspected—about Connor's adamant refusal to take over the role of Mr. Commitment in addition to taking over the medical practice. Unsurprised, Aiden offered what little advice he could come up with, which wasn't much because he echoed Connor's sentiment that Connor would make a terrible Mr. Commitment.

Connor was a smart, successful guy, but didn't have a clue about personal relationships. He never had.

"Dinner's ready," Jenny announced from the front door. Aiden patted his brother's shoulder and followed him back into the house.

Following the ingrained rule that his mom had established years before when she'd have five dirty kids running around, he and Connor washed up in the downstairs bath. They then made their way to the

large pecan table in the dining room that was used
only when they had a guest and on holidays.

Aiden sat down in his prescribed spot and was surprised to see Colleen enter the room with one of his
mom's flowered aprons wrapped around her, carrying
a large platter of roast beef. She'd pulled her hair back
in a bun, and her cheeks were flushed from the heat
of the kitchen.

She looked beautiful.

All at once, a rush of admiration filled him. She
looked so at home in this kind of Norman Rockwell
setting, so much a part of his family, so comfortable.

Was that an illusion? Would she ever be the kind
of woman who would be at ease in this sort of situation, or would her issues relating to her parents pre-
vent that?

Reminding himself that he shouldn't be dwelling
on Colleen's issues, or her ability to morph into a
domestic goddess when the need arose, he said,
"Looks like my mom really put you to work." He
quirked a smile.

She frowned slightly. "Your mom isn't feeling
well—"

"What do you mean?" he asked, concern leaping
to life in him.

Jenny stepped into the dining room, her blue-eyed,
towheaded daughter propped on her hip, and cut in
with, "Migraine."

Aiden blew out a breath and nodded, then waved
at his niece, who buried her face in her mom's neck.
For the last few years, blinding headaches that came

on with no warning had plagued his mother, and pretty much incapacitated her unless she slept for a few hours.

Jenny stuck a ladle in the gravy, then lowered Ava into the high chair next to her chair at the end of the table. "Mom went to bed, and since I can't cook worth beans, Colleen graciously took over and finished the dinner." She sat down. "She's quite the cook, you know."

He looked over the huge meal, which, in addition to the roast beef, included fresh steamed green beans, mashed potatoes and gravy, fluffy-looking biscuits and a colorful fruit salad. He knew that Colleen was a good cook, but even for her, this was a feat.

Amazed, he looked to Colleen, who had removed the apron to sit down next to Jenny. "You prepared this whole dinner, on the fly?"

She lifted a slender shoulder. "Not really. Your mom had everything ready to go. I just filled in at the end."

Jenny shook her head, smiled at their father as he seated himself at the head of the table, then turned her gaze back to Aiden. "Don't believe her. She whipped this meal into shape like a pro."

Aiden stared at Colleen. She'd willingly pitched in when needed and had become a part of his family with unexpected grace. A warmth filled his chest and appreciation sparked in him. She was something else. So much more fascinating than he'd expected.

Colleen sat happily talking and laughing about something Ava had done with Jenny, her blue eyes sparkling. He caught Colleen's gaze and smiled at her, but she just stared at him blankly for a second as if to say, "Remember, we don't mean anything to each other," and then went back to her conversation with Jenny.

Okay. Message received and acknowledged.

Suddenly, a vaguely sick feeling lurched through him, hollowing out his chest.

Weird. He should be relieved that she was distancing herself from him, that she posed less of a threat to his plans to have an unchallenging, uncomplicated life.

But he wasn't relieved. Instead, her withdrawal had left him feeling empty, lonely and incomplete.

Definitely not what he'd been going for.

Chapter Eight

Later that night, Colleen helped Jenny put Ava to bed. Then, after an entertaining round of charades that the women handily won even though the men outnumbered them three to two, she and Jenny took care of the dessert dishes, having an in-depth discussion about Ava's vocabulary.

Colleen then said good-night to everybody, carefully avoiding Aiden's penetrating, green gaze. Doing her best to ignore his eyes as they followed her, she found Molly and her baby in their bed in the kitchen, cuddled both of them for a few minutes to make herself feel better, and then headed for the guest room on the far end of the second floor.

As she walked down the hardwood hallway, she congratulated herself on keeping her distance from Aiden. She'd managed to stop herself from indulging in any more fantasies about being a part of his life and that of this warmhearted family.

She stepped into the guest room. It had been decorated in Victorian fashion, complete with elegant, yellow-flowered wallpaper, walnut bedroom suite with marble-topped dresser and nightstand, and a rich hand-woven, yellow-and-green rug underneath the bed. The butter-colored comforter was filled with goose down, and the matching pillowcases were embellished with delicate crocheting.

It was a cozy, welcoming room, the kind she'd always dreamed of having when she'd shared a tiny, drab room with her three foster sisters. Surprisingly, she immediately felt comfortable and at ease here— more than she'd imagined she would, given the circumstances.

After she changed into her pajamas and removed her makeup and brushed her teeth in the adjoining bath, she climbed into the soft bed, turned the light out and closed her eyes.

But sleep wouldn't come. With the quiet night, her vow to scour Aiden from her mind exploded into smithereens. All she could think about was their kiss and how much she wanted it to happen again. Pretty soon, her mind had her imagining that she could somehow change the flaw that lay deep inside her, allowing them to be together forever.

She sat bolt upright, snorting. That dim-witted thought chased away the desire to sleep. Grumbling, she threw off the covers and got out of bed. She needed air and time to work herself back to the I-can-never-love-Aiden place she needed to be.

Maybe she'd regain her unreliable sanity along the way.

After she carefully belted her cotton robe around her waist, she crept from her room and headed down to the porch. She stepped through the unlocked front door—only to find Aiden standing at the porch railing, staring into space, his broad-shouldered body dappled in shadows.

Her heart leaped, even though he was the last person she wanted to deal with right now.

Her lip clamped between her teeth, she ducked back inside, but he must have heard her. He swung around and saw her before she could close the door.

"Colleen," he said, smiling, his green eyes as dark as the sea at midnight. "Don't go."

Those softly spoken words zinged straight to her heart and rocked her world, and she hated herself for that clueless, idiotic reaction.

Deal with it. He probably just wanted to talk about the article.

She took a deep breath and let it out, calming her hyper nerves, then stepped out onto the porch, her bare feet silent on the cool wood. Balling her hands into fists, she told herself she could do this, had to do it. She needed to prove to herself that she was capable of shutting Aiden out, of dealing with him for her job.

"We need to talk," he said, stepping near, bringing his appealing scent with him.

She moved around him, not meeting his probing gaze, crossing her arms over her chest. "About what?" she asked, trying not to breathe.

"Earlier today, you said you'd put yourself somewhere." He stared at her. "What did you mean?"

She bit her lip, wishing he would just drop this subject and leave her alone. She didn't want to dwell on how hard it was to be around his perfect family, how unperfect her family was.

Unable to help herself, she looked at him. His spiky hair was mussed, and he had dark circles under his eyes. He looked really concerned.

All right. Maybe he did deserve an answer after the time they'd spent together, after what he'd done for her at Sun Mountain. And, really, what would it hurt? After this weekend, they would never see each other again.

She took a deep breath and let it out, working up her courage. "I meant that I wasn't interested in putting myself here," she indicated with a wave of her hand. "In the middle of your perfect family."

He looked perplexed, which made sense. His ideal, wonderful family wasn't unusual or anything special by his standards. Just by hers, thanks to her twisted parents.

"So being here...bothers you?"

She shifted on her feet, then abruptly moved over and sat at the table, giving in to her Jell-O-like knees. "Yes, it does."

He lowered his big, wonderful-smelling body into

the chair next to her. "Why?" he softly asked. "Everyone's been nice to you, haven't they?"

To her utter horror, she felt tears burning in her eyes. His family had welcomed her with open arms and had treated her as if they'd known her forever, something her own parents had never come close to. "Of course." She looked away. "That's the problem."

Out of the corner of her eye, she saw him frown. "How can someone being nice to you be a problem?"

He was never going to leave her alone about this unless she leveled with him, and she wanted this conversation, and his probing, over with as quickly as possible. She forced herself to say, "Because then it'll be harder not to care."

He sat back in his chair, shaking his head. "And you don't want to care because…" He trailed off, clearly expecting her to finish his sentence. But before she could, he leaned forward and said, "Because of your parents. They didn't love you…so you don't want to care about anybody else?"

She simply nodded, thankful he'd pretty much figured out her problem on his own, except the part about not *wanting* to love anybody else. It went so much deeper than that, related more to her flaw and inability to love another living thing. It was difficult to verbally admit that she didn't have a clue how to act around a family or that the prospect of having to deal with caring about another person terrified her.

Or that if she cared it would hurt so much more to

lose what she cared about. She'd cared about her parents, and they'd deserted her. It didn't get much more painful than that.

He stood and began to pace the porch. "So let me get this straight. You're afraid to care about my family." He pinned her in place with his hardening green gaze. "Do I have that right?"

"That sums it up, yes."

He stared at her, then gave her a soft, comforting smile. "Honey, do you have any idea how ridiculous that is?"

She bristled, even though she foolishly loved that he'd called her honey. "It is not."

He sat back down. "Yes, it is. You're using the excuse of your wounded childhood to keep from having to risk your heart, to risk caring about another person."

Oh-ho. That loaded comment deserved a comeback. And, boy, did she have one. "You're one to talk," she said, rising. "I see the shadows in your eyes and the lines on your face. Obviously something has affected you deeply, but you won't talk about it, won't even acknowledge it. You're running away from something, just like I am. At least I have the guts to admit it."

He stared at her, his eyes flat and emotionless—too emotionless—his hand clenched into a fist at his side. Clearly, he was doing his best, again, to cover up how he really felt, to keep his demons at bay, or maybe pretend they didn't exist. "You don't know what you're talking about," he intoned.

"Oh, yes, I do." She stood and went to the railing, looking out at the flower-filled yard—the kind of play area she'd dreamed about as a child—illuminated by the light of the moon. "Believe me, I know all about running away." She'd run away from him eight years ago. She was an expert on that.

He was silent for a long moment. "Maybe you do. But you didn't run away today, did you? You jumped in and helped out like you were part of this family."

She scoffed. "That was no big deal."

"For you, it was. You just told me how hard it is for you to be in the midst of my family, but you're doing just fine."

She considered his words but didn't believe them. She didn't do "family" any more than she did "relationship," and had failed at being part of her parents' world. "I cooked dinner, Aiden, that's all. That didn't take any special skill except knowing how to operate the oven."

He took her hand in his, sending shivers through her body. "You're so blind," he said, his mouth curved into a half smile that made her heart race. "You're better at this family stuff than you think."

She stared at him, loving the chiseled planes of his face and how his eyes caressed her. Oh, how she wished she could take what he'd said to heart and embrace the concept of being part of a family. But a cold, empty, doubtful place inside her wouldn't let her. And that made her incredibly sad.

Her eyes burning, she pulled her hand from his, needing to keep her distance, needing to back away from the tempting, wonderful man in front of her and the threat he represented.

A threat that she would be a fool not to heed.

"No, I'm not blind," she said, shaking her head. "Just smart."

He opened his mouth to speak, but she raised her hands and ruthlessly cut him off. "Don't say anything else. None of this matters, Aiden, because after this weekend, you and I won't be seeing each other again."

He stared at her, his eyes hardening. "I agree with you, but I'm curious about your reasoning. Why not?" he asked, his words echoing in the dark.

This was important to get out on the table. There had to be no mistaking what had to happen, what she needed to do to stay safe. "Because we're…hopeless." She took a shuddering breath. "I might get along just fine with your wonderful family, but I don't know how to love any more than I did eight years ago."

He pressed his lips into a hard line, stood and glared at her. "You really believe that, don't you?"

Her eyes still burning, all she could do was nod.

He abruptly moved to the porch railing, his back to her, his hands shoved into his pockets. "Well, then you're right. We're hopeless. We always were."

She stared at his broad back, a crushing disappointment filling her.

Because, while she believed what she'd said with everything in her, she was horrified to realize now that she'd still stupidly hoped deep down inside that he would somehow be able to make the burning, painful truth go away.

That he would care enough about her to convince her that she was wrong.

But neither was true.

Mercy. Why did she always do this to herself? Why did she let herself hold on to the fantasy that she would ever be whole enough to love him or that he could somehow magically make her flaw disappear?

Her heart crumbling, she silently turned and walked back into the house, leaving Aiden on the porch by himself.

Leaving her foolish dreams in the dust where they belonged.

Then next morning, after barely sleeping at all, Colleen was awakened by the smell of brewing coffee and fragrant baking pastry she pegged as cinnamon rolls.

Her stomach rumbling, she quickly showered and dressed in a pair of olive-green pants, a white tank top and Keds, then went downstairs to the kitchen, thankful the men had left before dawn, as planned the night before, to go fishing. A quiet morning without Aiden around, reminding her of their late-night conversation and her crushed dreams, was just what she needed. Hopefully, she could get some work on ''The Baby Chronicles'' done and find out about the pictures Joe wanted.

Molly and her puppy greeted her, and she couldn't resist squatting and petting both for a few moments, enjoying their soft, curly fur and adoring, coal-black eyes.

She rose, noticing Aiden's mom and sister sitting at the oak kitchen table, huge, steaming coffee cups nearby, a large platter of cinnamon rolls in the middle of the table. They had black-and-white pictures spread out in front of them.

The pictures Joe wanted?

Both women looked up, smiling.

"Good morning," Jenny said, pushing a lock of her blond hair behind her ear. "Grab a cup of coffee, have a roll, and join us before Ava wakes up and the peace and quiet ends." She gestured to the coffee-maker on the counter near the sink.

Marveling at how easily these women welcomed her into their home, Colleen said, "Good morning. Those rolls smell delicious."

"Mom's secret recipe. If you get on her good side, maybe she'll share it with you."

Mrs. Forbes smiled, the skin around her hazel eyes crinkling. "I'd be happy to give you the recipe. From what I hear, you're a fantastic cook."

The compliment, coming from Aiden's mother, filled Colleen with glowing pride. "You did most of the work. I just tied the loose ends together." She poured a cup of hot coffee. "Are you feeling better, Mrs. Forbes?"

"Yes, dear, I am, thank you," she said. "And please call me Sheila."

Coffee cup in hand, Colleen walked over to the table, set her mug down and helped herself to a warm cinnamon roll. She sat down next to Sheila, her stomach twisting. If these were the photos Joe wanted, was now the time to talk to Sheila about them? "Pictures?"

Sheila nodded. "Aiden took these while he was overseas."

Bingo. Colleen looked at the thirty or so black-and-white pictures spread on the table, her breath catching in her throat. "Oh, mercy," she murmured.

The pictures were of babies and toddlers, dark-eyed waifs who were clearly poverty-ridden, clothed—if they had clothes on at all—in rags. Some of the children were pictured in front of desolate bombed-out buildings, and some in nomadic tentlike structures. Despite the horrific subject matter, they were beautifully photographed using shadow and light, haunting in their very nature.

She swallowed and turned her gaze to Sheila, her appetite suddenly gone. "These are heartbreaking."

"Yes, they are." Her eyes reflecting a deep sadness, she picked up one and studied it, tracing the baby's face with her finger. "I don't know how Aiden dealt with photographing this kind of stuff for so long. It's obvious he saw things like this every day."

Photographing this…

Understanding clicked into place in Colleen's mind. Now that she'd seen the graphic kinds of things he'd dealt with and lived through, it wasn't hard to comprehend what had etched the lines in his face and put shadows in his eyes.

He'd slogged through hell.

She pushed away the cinnamon roll. Funny. She'd always pictured him as the dashing photojournalist, traveling the world in glamorous style, snapping pictures here and there. It had been easy to maintain that glamorous, innocuous image in her mind because she'd deliberately avoided looking at his work.

Her image had been so off base. So wrong.

He'd witnessed the kind of horror that turned innocent children into starving, rag-clad sticks with bulging bellies and despair-filled eyes.

Her heart broke for him. It was little wonder he was so anxious to become a baby photographer and take pictures of healthy, glowing babies.

And she had to admit, now that she'd seen the photographs, Joe was right. These pictures were graphically haunting and would give an added depth and dimension to "The Baby Chronicles." "Did Aiden give these pictures to you?"

Sheila nodded and picked up the envelope with the word *Mom* scribbled across the front. "The day after he returned, he grimly handed this envelope to me and told me to get rid of it. I got the impression he didn't want to see them ever again." She frowned slightly, considering one of the photos. "But I think he should."

"Why?" Colleen asked, extremely curious about Sheila's reasoning. It might clue Colleen in as to whether the woman would be willing to have them published.

Sheila wrapped her hands around the large, flowered coffee mug sitting on the table in front of her, a sad smile on her lightly lined face. "He just wants to forget what he saw, bury it and move on. Personally, I think that's a mistake. But then again, that's Aiden—forge ahead, don't look back."

Colleen couldn't agree more. She firmly believed Aiden was simply trying to blot out his horrible memories rather than deal with them.

She looked back to Sheila. "What do you think about publishing these pictures in 'The Baby Chronicles,' juxtaposed next to the photos of healthy babies Aiden took at Sun Mountain?" She looked to Sheila and then to Jenny, taking a sip of coffee. "It would be a touching, thought-provoking piece, and might also boost Aiden's career, which I know is important to him."

"And it might force him to deal with what he experienced rather than running away from it," Sheila said, tilting her head to the side. "A bit sneaky, but definitely effective."

"So you think it's a good idea?" Colleen asked.

Sheila nodded slowly. "I think I do."

"Do I have your permission to publish them?"

"You do."

Colleen turned to Jenny. "And what do you think?"

Jenny took a sip of coffee and smiled, her hazel eyes sparkling. "I think it's a great idea. Just be prepared for the fur to fly when Aiden finds out. He's as stubborn as an old goat, and he doesn't want to deal with those pictures even though he needs to."

Colleen forced a smile, suddenly even more apprehensive about this whole plan. More than likely, Jenny was right on. When Aiden found out what she, Colleen, had done, the fur would probably explode in her face.

She couldn't let herself think about that. She firmly believed Aiden needed to see these pictures to heal, and she was sure that publishing them would be good for his career. That aside, Joe wanted them. Reason enough to go ahead and call him.

She excused herself to call Joe on her cell phone to tell him she had the pictures. Their conversation was brief; he was ecstatic and needed the pictures right away to make the printing deadline.

After she told Sheila and Jenny she was returning to Portland to deliver the photos, she convinced them to agree not to tell Aiden exactly why she'd left, coming up with a story about a late-breaking assignment, although he would undoubtedly figure it all out when he saw the new, improved article. Colleen then returned to the guest room, gathered her things and packed her bag.

Ten minutes later, she said a sad farewell to the two poodles, a lump in her throat, then waved goodbye to Sheila and Jenny as they stood on the porch. She drove away feeling strangely conflicted. Why was her heart aching when she should be relieved to be getting away from all of this…connectedness?

On her way back to Portland she had an attack of conscience that deflated her determination to see the pictures as part of the spread. Yes, it would be a touching, significant piece with the photos included.

But she couldn't ignore the truth. She had no business betraying Aiden like this.

She turned around and headed back toward Oak Valley, her nerves on full alert, knowing her choice might cost her her job. The only comfort she found was that at least this way there was a chance it wouldn't cost her Aiden's respect.

Sheila was understanding. "Colleen," she said, putting a warm hand on Colleen's arm. "Don't worry about this."

Colleen gave her a nervous glance. "I'll try, but my editor wants these photos. I'd like to supply them, but just can't betray Aiden like that. Jenny's right. He'd be furious."

Sheila smiled wryly. "That may be true, but I think publishing them will help in the long run. So don't you worry about a thing." She held out a hand. "I'll see that your editor gets the pictures right away, and you don't have to be involved at all."

Surprised, Colleen stared at Sheila, then handed over the packet. "You're willing to do that?"

"Of course. He'll be angry, but he'll get over it." She looked to Jenny. "Are you and Ava up for a trip to Portland?"

Colleen pressed a hand to her stomach, wishing she hadn't become involved in any of this. And while Sheila would be the one to actually hand over the pictures, Colleen still felt somewhat responsible for the whole thing since she'd come here under false pretenses, specifically for the photographs, and because she'd brought up the idea in the first place, at

Joe's behest. Now she wished she'd just kept quiet, even though that would have been risky if she wanted to remain employed.

Sheila invited her to stay for the rest of the weekend, but Colleen declined. Her guilt ate at her, prompting a need to be alone, and things between her and Aiden had become too complicated. She just wanted to go home and complete "The Baby Chronicles" on her own, in her protected little world, safe from Aiden's influence.

As she drove home, she couldn't help but think about one thing: she might be safe from his influence, but given the part she'd played in getting the photos printed, she still wasn't safe from losing his respect.

The next morning, Aiden awakened, still disappointed that Colleen had left to take care of a late-breaking story before he'd returned from the Forbes men's fishing expedition. He'd thought of her constantly while he'd fished the McKenzie River, remembering her smiles and laughter the night before, how she'd taken to Jenny, Ava and the dogs.

He'd discovered a new, wonderful side to her in the last few days, a part of her he couldn't help but admire, an endearing, unexpected facet he wanted to explore.

He sat on the bed, shaking his head. That idea was insane. He and Colleen had crashed and burned eight years ago, and he didn't want to live through that kind of pain again, not to mention that Colleen represented a challenge he didn't want to face.

But he had to admit, she'd changed enough to spend time with his family in Oak Valley, something he suspected she never could have accomplished when they'd been dating before. In fact, he'd always had the impression that she'd avoided meeting his family.

As he pulled on his clothes, cautious hope grew in him. Colleen had blossomed here, shed part of her shell, and somehow turned into the kind of woman he might be able to get lost in all over again.

And that scared the hell out of him.

That was the grim but necessary reality he had to concentrate on. He ruthlessly shoved his ludicrous hopes back in their hole where they belonged, then finished dressing, focusing instead on the anticipation coming to life inside of him. "The Baby Chronicles," his first and maybe most important foray into baby photography, was appearing in today's paper. He was excited to see how his pictures of healthy, blooming-with-life babies looked in newsprint.

Since his parents didn't have a subscription to the *Beacon,* he was planning to walk downtown and pick up a copy at Mercer's Mercantile.

He popped his head into the kitchen, the aroma of a freshly cooked breakfast making his mouth water, sorry he wouldn't be able to enjoy his mom's regular Sunday-morning meal of Belgian waffles and sausage until he returned.

His mom and dad were sitting at the kitchen table, each enjoying a cup of coffee. His dad was dressed for the day in old jeans and the ancient Oregon Ducks

T-shirt he always wore when he did chores in the yard, his usual Sunday-morning activity. He had a giant, syrup-smothered plateful of waffles in front of him.

"Hey, guys," Aiden said. "I'm going to go down and pick up a copy of..." He trailed off when his eyes snagged on the newspaper on the table. "Is that a copy of the *Beacon*?"

His mom, still dressed in her perennial blue bathrobe, looked up and smiled. "Yes, it is. Your father picked up a copy. He was up with the roosters this morning."

Aiden moved into the kitchen, noticing that his dad wouldn't quite meet his gaze. "Oh. Good. Thanks." He rubbed his hands together, shrugging off his father's odd look. "So. How did 'The Baby Chronicles' turn out?"

His mom raised her chin. "It's wonderful." She turned to her husband. "What do you think, Brady?"

"Nice job," he said around a chunk of waffle, nodding sagely, a strange look reflected in his green eyes.

Aiden frowned, sensing something was up. His dad was a social talker by nature, the habit meshing perfectly with his role as Mr. Commitment. He usually had a lot more to say than a two-word response.

Lowering his eyebrows, a bad feeling creeping up on him, Aiden slowly picked up the Living section off the top of the pile.

When he looked down, half holding his breath at what he might find, surprise exploded like a nuclear bomb inside him.

Instead of healthy, chubby, gorgeous babies, the images from his nightmares leaped off the page at him.

Starving, bloated babies, staring back at him, cold, numb despair and lost hope emanating from their dark, pleading eyes.

Terrible memories rose up in his brain like a tide of acid, tearing him apart, opening old wounds, searing him from the inside out.

Death.

Poverty.

Dying children.

I couldn't help them.

A familiar, hated, sick feeling moved through him, tightening his belly. And the helplessness and rage and despair and guilt he'd felt every single day that he'd lived overseas reared up like a snarling dragon and threatened to eat him alive.

He closed his eyes, trying with everything in him to rein in his dark, ravaging memories. After a few long, agonizing moments, the sick feeling receded slightly, and he opened his eyes to hurriedly look over the rest of the piece. The pictures he'd taken at Sun Mountain, the life-affirming babies intended to be his salvation, were there, too, just as they were supposed to be.

But the other pictures…

No, no, no.

He crumpled the paper closed. He didn't bother to read the copy Colleen had written. He was too angry, feeling too betrayed to do that. Instead, he let the paper fall to the table and looked at his mom, tightening his jaw. "I gave those pictures to you. How did they get into the paper?"

She stubbornly lifted her chin again. "I gave them to your editor."

"You what?" he ground out, his lips barely moving. "Why?"

"Because I thought they needed to be printed. I thought it would be good for you to face your horrible memories rather than ignoring them."

Damn, but that sounded just like his mom. She was one of the most practical, grounded, emotionally healthy people he knew. In that light, it wasn't hard to see why she'd done this, even though her meddling bugged the hell out of him. "You had no right to publish those pictures."

"I had every right. You gave them to me. I want what's best for you, and what's best is for you to face those images. You can't just bury your head in the sand, you know."

Man, he hated that his mom was pushing him on this. He was dealing with his searing past and its horrific memories the best, the *only,* way he knew how. He looked to his father for support. "Dad?"

His dad regarded him with solemn eyes. "She's right, Son. You're running away from what haunts you rather than facing it down."

Aiden stood silently. They were dead wrong. He knew his parents loved him, but hated that they would cut him off at the knees like this, forcing him to look at things that he wanted to forget.

Letting out a heavy breath, he asked, "So did my editor call you and ask for them?" He vividly remembered Joe wanting more pictures the first time Aiden had met with him and Colleen in Joe's office.

A pained look crossed his mom's face. "Uh, well…not exactly."

Aiden peered at her, uneasy with her odd expression. "Well, how *exactly* did he get them?"

His mother pursed her lips but remained silent.

Before Aiden could speak, his dad piped up with, "Oh, hell, this is ridiculous, Sheila. Tell him the truth."

She leaned in to his father and said in a low voice, "But I promised her—"

"Promised who?" Aiden drilled. All at once, the truth dawned on him like a sudden, icy downpour. *Her* had to be Colleen.

Colleen had come here to engineer all of this.

Hot, blinding anger rose in him. Colleen had told him she needed help on "The Baby Chronicles," but what she'd really wanted to do was meddle in his life. His parents had merely agreed to what Colleen had wheedled her way in here to get.

Damn her. He wanted, *needed,* to forget the horrors connected with those photos, and she had stirred up all kinds of searing memories by asking his mother to agree to print them.

He wheeled around. "I gotta go."

He heard his parents call to him, but he ignored them and, to their credit, they let him go. Without stopping, he pulled his car keys from the brass hook shaped like an F near the front door and stomped out of the house.

A few minutes later he left Oak Valley, driving faster than he should, the slow burn of his previous anger building like a banked fire in him.

As he drove the almost deserted roads that led to the highway, two questions spun round and round in his mind.

When was Colleen going to stop hurting him?

And when was he going to stop letting her close enough to do damage?

He pressed the accelerator, his hands gripping the steering wheel.

The damage would stop right here. Right now.

For good.

Chapter Nine

Colleen hefted a stack of brimming file folders onto her desk, blowing her hair out of her face. The mess that was her office was out of control, and she was sick of facing the dump every day. So, she'd decided to come in on Sunday and sort through the huge piles surrounding her desk, to go with the unexpected positive flow and motivation and begin to clean up her life, starting slow and easy with her office.

A girl could only take on so much change at one time.

She waded through the office mess, smiling despite the fact that she and Aiden had parted on a negative note. ''The Baby Chronicles'' had turned out beautifully. Adding the pictures Aiden's mother had delivered to Joe had given the article a heart-tugging, intensely touching dimension.

Apparently, Joe shared her opinion. He'd called her late last night, raving about how well the whole thing had come together and about how the haunting black-and-white pictures had contrasted so well with the playful color photos Aiden had taken at Sun Mountain. He'd also complimented her on the modified copy she'd hastily pounded out, which had explained and expounded upon the significance of the two sets of pictures.

The piece had gone from a fluffy pictorial on cute babies to a profoundly touching commentary on what was wrong with a world in which babies were left to suffer.

Hopefully Aiden would see the spread in a positive light.

She shoved away the nagging suspicion that she was kidding herself in a major way. By his mother's admission, he was stuck in his usual, infuriating "full speed ahead and ignore the bad things in his past" mode. She doubted he would relish looking at those photos, even though he needed to.

"What the hell did you think you were doing?"

Startled, she jerked her head up. As if she'd conjured him up from her dire thoughts, Aiden stood in the door of her half-cleaned cube, his eyes blazing green fire. He looked as good as he always did, his body tall, lean and masculine, which she knew from experience was a perfect fit for hers. Yes, he even looked good with his spiky hair sticking out at funny angles, looking as if it hadn't seen a shower yet this morning. He looked mussed and hot and so darn good.

Before she could get her mind off how wonderful he looked, even though he was, obviously, hopping mad, he stalked closer and stopped in front of her desk. "Dammit, Colleen. You had no right to convince my mom to publish those pictures."

He crossed his arms over his broad, T-shirt-covered chest and pressed his mouth into a hard, grim line. He pulled his eyebrows low over his eyes and glared at her.

Mercy. He was furious. More furious than she'd ever seen him.

Her stomach dropped. A dull ache filled her chest.

Obviously, she'd made a major mistake by going to his mother about the pictures. In hindsight, faced with his steaming anger, she wished she'd thought this through a little more, wished she'd put a little more importance on how Aiden would react.

But there it was—her flaw rearing its ugly, predictable head. If she'd had a clue about relationships, she would have instinctively known how mad he'd be about this, she would have been more tuned in to his feelings.

She would have known how detrimental publishing the pictures would be, no matter who was responsible for it.

Instead, she'd charged ahead, all in the name of healing Aiden and helping his career.

Ha! Judging by the livid look on his face, whether

he was healed or not wasn't going to make any difference.

She was toast in his eyes.

So be it. No matter what he thought of her, she was determined to show him how much he needed those pictures published.

Aiden grimly wrapped his anger around him like a flak jacket, needing it to ignore the wounded expression on Colleen's face, and how gorgeous she looked in the tight lime-green shirt she wore. He didn't want to feel sorry for her, or let the hurt in her pretty, blue eyes get to him, or let her beauty derail him from saying what needed to be said.

He'd done that too many times before and he'd always been the one to suffer the pain in the end. Hell, he'd let her walk out on him eight years ago without calling her on it. No, instead, he'd run away, straight into hell, straight into the horrific memories that burning place had charred onto his soul.

Not this time. She'd meddled in his life and damn if he wasn't going to call her on what she'd done.

Leaning down, he pressed his hands on the top of her desk and demanded, "Well?"

She took a deep breath, then turned determined blue eyes up to him. "Why are you so angry? The piece turned out wonderfully. Even Joe thought so. This could do wonders for your career as a baby photographer."

He wheeled around, away from her. "This isn't about my career—"

"Since when?" she said, cutting him off. "Your whole focus has been on your career since you returned from overseas."

I wish. Despite his common sense screaming at him, he'd focused way too much time on Colleen since he'd been back. And, damn, was he paying the price in pain now.

He nodded, though, inclining his head, not about to share any of that with her, to let her know how much power he'd given her. "You're right. I wanted to concentrate on photographing babies. And that was going along pretty good. 'The Baby Chronicles' was the perfect way for me to launch the career I want."

He clenched his hands into fists. "But this isn't about that. This is about the *new* 'Baby Chronicles,' which wasn't the story I had in mind. God knows I didn't want any reminders of…" He trailed off. Could he really share with her his terrible memories? Could he possibly open himself up to the searing pain and guilt he felt whenever he thought about what he'd witnessed—and walked away from, not able to help?

She put a hand on his arm and the scent of peaches washed over him. "Reminders of what?"

He shook his head and pulled away from her warm, mesmerizing touch and alluring scent, unable to reveal—and face—the wrenching horrors and guilt that had infested his entire being.

"Reminders of what you saw?" she asked in a soft, compelling voice.

Twisting agony rose up in him. How could anybody really forget—or discuss—starving, dying babies,

babies he couldn't save? Those images and his failure were simply too horrible to contemplate while he had a choice. But when he was asleep, without control, the nightmares would come, tearing him apart, bit by bit by bit.

All he could do was nod.

"Oh, Aiden. I know you're upset that those heart-breaking pictures were printed."

He clenched his jaw. "I wanted to forget what those pictures represent, and you've brought it all back."

"But don't you see? You want to forget and surround yourself with innocence and light in hopes that the icky stuff will just go away." She paused and turned away. "But trust me, it won't work."

He jerked his gaze to her slim back. "Why is that?"

She shrugged her shoulders and let them drop. "You've said some things that were difficult for me to face. I admit I have icky stuff in my past, too—granted, not as bad as what you've gone through. But I've been trying to deal with that, and you've shown me that I've used my childhood as an excuse not to risk my heart." She turned around, her blue eyes piercing. "We've both been doing the same thing, even though we went about it in different ways. I used my past as an excuse not to love. You're avoiding dealing with your past, which is keeping you from the real world now."

"The real world?" he said harshly. He'd lived through major real, complete with all the devastating ravages of war. "I saw the real world, a world where babies died in front of me, where whole families were wiped out by bombs and I couldn't do anything to save them. Don't you dare tell me I don't know the real world. I know it too damn well."

"I get that, Aiden, and trust me, I'm not trying to minimize what you went through. But burying your past and living an engineered life filled with sweet, innocent things isn't the real world in the here and now."

Hell, he didn't want to deal with any of this. Pain and guilt were waiting for him if he did. And why in the hell was she challenging him on this, anyway? She usually ran away from these kinds of conversations. She'd even admitted on the porch the other day that she was an expert on cutting out when things got tough.

Whatever her reasons, she picked the wrong thing to get personal with.

He moved to the door of her office. He now realized that it was time to finish the roll of film that was him and Colleen. This was over.

"You're wrong, Colleen. I haven't buried my past, I've simply moved on," he said. "And I've got to move on now. I don't think I can ever forgive you for starting the ball rolling on publishing those pictures without discussing it with me first. Hell, you even lied about your reason for coming to my parents' just to get to those photos."

She stared at him for a long time, tears shimmering in her blue eyes, and an astounding thought occurred to him. Had she been hoping for a love-filled future with him?

Oh, man. He certainly hadn't expected that, given she thought she didn't know how to love. Even so, her wish had come eight years too late and her meddling had permanently killed any chance of a future for them.

And he couldn't be the man she so obviously wanted—one who could step back into hell and relive the horrors that had shaped him into the tormented person he was today.

A man who would get over how much she'd hurt him, not eight years ago, but right now, with the pictures.

Not knowing what to say, he turned to go, needing space. Needing the peace of forgetting what he'd witnessed. He knew now that Colleen would never let him do that.

He couldn't see her anymore. Ever.

Her voice stopped him. "You'll never be truly happy and healed until you face your past, you know."

He bent his head, considering her words, then discarding them. His past was just that—passed. "You've got it all wrong, Colleen. I'll never be happy if I *do* face my past." He turned his head and snagged her gaze. "Obviously I can't be the man you need now."

I never was.

A lone tear ran down her cheek, and the sight hit him like a rock. Colleen rarely opened up enough to allow herself to cry. She *was* different. But it was too late to matter.

Raw, stupid hope rose inside him, but he whacked it down, reminding himself that the price he would pay to be with Colleen was too high and he wouldn't, *couldn't,* pay it again. Repeating that to himself over and over, he forced himself to turn from her lovely face and walk away. He was doing the right thing.

He left the building and walked to his car, thinking about the life that loomed before him, the life he'd just made for himself. He would never hear Colleen laugh again, never see her sparkling blue eyes, never hold her in his arms again and breathe in her peachy scent.

He would never see her hold their baby.

A dull spot formed in his heart, a hollow, aching place.

And damn, even though he hated the thought, he couldn't help but wonder if he hadn't simply traded one kind of pain for another.

Aiden was gone.

Numb, Colleen looked at the space he'd just occupied in her office, regretting the loss of his presence as she'd never regretted anything before.

Mercy, she saw now, in hindsight, that she'd hoped that he would love her!

Get real, Colleen. Aiden had baggage of his own— enough, she'd sadly discovered, to fill an ocean liner—that made a relationship impossible.

It was glaringly obvious that she couldn't be fixed

any more than Aiden could be fixed. Her inherent inability to love, to nurture a relationship, had created a distance between them that couldn't be bridged.

She still didn't have a clue about being part of a healthy romantic relationship. She'd done the totally wrong thing by setting up the situation that had allowed those pictures to be printed, and had driven Aiden away.

A chill ran up her spine. That sounded familiar.

She could see now that she'd done the same thing eight years ago by intentionally sabotaging their relationship. Granted, her actions now hadn't been to intentionally ruin things between them. She'd actually hoped that forcing Aiden to face his past via the pictures would help heal him so he could be whole.

But that wasn't the entire problem.

Her flaw ran so deep that *she* was just as big a part of the problem. She should have instinctively known how painful printing those pictures would be to him. She should have wanted to protect him from his pain rather than forcing him to deal with things that he didn't want to deal with.

So, that was that. She and Aiden were through. Too many things stood between them to ever repair their relationship.

Her fantasy of having Aiden in her life was just that—a fantasy that would never come true.

That realization raised an almost unbearable pain inside her. Pressing a shaky hand to her mouth, she held in a sob, hating that she'd set herself up for this kind of turmoil.

And began Life After Aiden, Part 3.

Chapter Ten

Since he'd promised to help his mom in the yard with some backbreaking work he didn't want his dad doing, Aiden returned to his parents' house and spent the remainder of Sunday there. He was still furious at his mom for giving the photos to Joe, but she was his mom, after all, and he knew she had his best interests at heart. Of course, he would eventually forgive her.

He worked his tail off and did his best not to think about how achingly dead his heart felt, even though he had to deal with his family's pointed questions about Colleen. Hell, his father had even cornered him on the porch and put on his Mr. Commitment hat, attempting to apply his small-town brand of relationship remedy. Just about that time, Aiden had suddenly been struck with the burning desire to mow the lawn, knowing his father would probably follow him but couldn't be heard over the ancient lawn mower.

The next day Aiden returned home, and after spending a hellish night ruthlessly telling himself he'd done the right thing—the *only* thing he could have done—he went to the *Beacon* to meet with Joe, who'd called bright and early requesting a powwow.

Aiden went directly to Joe's office, hoping he wouldn't run into Colleen. The dull ache that still throbbed inside him every time he thought about a life without her was still too fresh for him to face her yet.

No, walking away from Colleen wasn't something he wanted to analyze or discuss with anyone.

It was past. Over. Done with.

In his usual way, he wanted to just box it all neatly up and move on. Didn't hurt so much that way.

Joe hailed him when he walked into his office. "Hey, Aiden. Thanks for coming." He gestured to the metal chair across from his desk. "Have a seat."

Aiden lowered himself into the chair. "What's up, Joe?" He'd prudently decided not to make waves with Joe for pushing so hard for the photos since he was, in essence, his boss, and could help make or break his initial success as a baby photographer.

Joe smiled and held up a copy of "The Baby Chronicles." "This is what's up. Way up. The response to your pictures has been phenomenal. We've had calls from people who want to donate money to help these kids, calls from those who want to adopt them, calls complimenting the sensitivity and note-worthiness of the feature.''

Shock rolled through Aiden. He'd been so trau-matized when he'd taken the pictures he hadn't stopped to consider that they might have some value other than to torment him. He'd just wanted to get rid of them.

And even though he hated the article for what it represented in his life, he would be a heartless fool not to be glad the doctored version of the spread had gone over well and had inspired interest in needy chil-dren. ''That's great, Joe, but what does that have to do with me?''

Joe took a sip of coffee from a battered coffee cup with a picture of an old typewriter on it. ''Because of the article's success, I'd like to do another. You game?''

Aiden inclined his head, considering. More new pictures in the paper *would* be good for his career. Old photos—he shuddered inside—forget it. ''That depends. I'd love to take more pictures on loca-tion—''

Joe shook his head. ''Not what I'm after.'' He leaned forward, lifting his bushy, gray eyebrows. ''I want more of those black-and-white pictures you took overseas.''

Damn those pictures. Dread crawled through Aiden like a big, disgusting slug. The last thing he wanted to do was bring out more pictures and dredge up more painful memories.

And damn Colleen, too. This complication was another unwanted ramification of her meddling.

He adamantly shook his head, but before he could let loose with a hearty "no way," a woman spoke from behind Aiden.

"Joe, Mr. Parker has moved your meeting up without any notice. He's waiting for you now."

Joe stood. "That's the big boss calling." He grabbed a folder from his desk and moved toward the door. "This'll be great exposure for you, and I'm sure you'll jump at the chance to show off your work. What better way to get attention and have something good come of what you've photographed?" He shoved the folder under his arm and yanked his loosened tie tight. "No-brainer, right? Collect up those photos right away. I'd like them to appear in the Living section that runs on Wednesday, day after tomorrow, so I'll need them pronto."

Without a look back, or an answer from Aiden, Joe hustled his rotund body out the door, leaving Aiden sitting in the office, his jaw slack, anger burning like an exploded missile inside him.

No-brainer.

Right.

Obviously, Joe thought it was a given that Aiden was willing to publish more of those pictures. The guy had blithely walked out, confident enough in Aiden's answer to not even hang around for his response.

Aiden stood, shaking his head. Why didn't anybody else understand that it was a big deal to look at those photos, to remember the suffering children he'd seen, the relentless guilt that burned inside him, never letting him rest? Everybody else, from his mother to Colleen to Joe, seemed to think he should be able to deal with all that.

He pinched the bridge of his nose.

Get real, Forbes. You're living in a fantasy world.

That thought bugged the hell out of him. Made him feel powerless.

But even though he hated being forced to do something that he instinctively knew would be agonizing, he'd been forced to see that he couldn't easily bury and ignore his memories and experiences forever.

Sure, he wanted to ignore everybody's unwanted advice, and had for the last few days. Since he'd come home, really. But he'd always thought of himself as a pretty sensible, reasonable kind of guy, at least before his soul-ripping stint overseas.

Maybe he finally needed to listen to the people who cared about him.

His stomach twisting, he went over to the window and gazed, unseeing, out of the small window in back of Joe's desk. This was the here and now, and whether he liked it or not, he had to face reality. He was beginning to realize that publishing the photos might actually help the children he hadn't been able to save. That was positive and might appease his guilt, something that had never occurred to him, given the personally traumatic nature of the photos.

Second, obviously the pictures were creating a stir,

which would undoubtedly be good for his career as a baby photographer.

He turned from the window. Actually, viewed in that light, including the pictures had actually turned out all right, even though it had been like stepping back into his nightmares to see them...

A hot chill swept up his spine.

Colleen had been right. She'd known what he needed and made it happen.

He sat down in Joe's chair, his knees suddenly weak.

Colleen is the best thing that has ever happened to me.

The thought exploded in his mind with the force of a land mine, and he realized that helping the kids in the pictures and the success of his business, while very worthwhile, weren't the most important result of what Colleen had done.

Colleen's actions had shown him that he *could* handle the challenge she represented.

And that was *huge*. He'd fought wanting Colleen for a long time, and he'd latched on to her "betrayal" to help him do that. But there it was—the truth, impossible to ignore.

He wanted Colleen.

Raw, razor-sharp anxiety knifed through him.

He'd have to look his past in the eye to have her. She'd forced him to realize and accept that. A bolt of admiration and respect hurtled through him.

He thought of Colleen's generous smile, how wonderful she was with little Laura, how much she'd helped him on the photo shoot at Sun Mountain, how she'd jumped feetfirst into his family and earned her place in it even though that had terrified her.

She was an amazing woman. She always had been. He hadn't fallen for her eight years ago for nothing.

You want to forget and surround yourself with innocence and light in hopes that the icky stuff will just go away.

Her wise words echoed in his head and he forced himself to look inward, something he hadn't done for a very long time.

Maybe never.

Ah, damn. She was right. He'd returned from overseas filled with terrible, searing memories and guilt that he wanted to eradicate from his brain by focusing on things like healthy, life-affirming babies and a rosy, picture-perfect life with an unchallenging woman.

A woman who wouldn't force him to look too deeply inside.

It had been so easy to keep his feelings for Colleen at bay by immediately deciding that because she didn't fit into the life he wanted, she wasn't the woman for him. He'd been using his fantasy of an ideal existence as a shield against Colleen because she challenged the hell out of him.

But he saw now that fabricating a life to avoid dealing with the unpleasantness of his past was wrong…and pretty stupid. Freed from those limits it was easy to see the truth.

I love her. Still.

The thought should have surprised him, but didn't. He'd suspected, deep down in a place he'd shut off, that he loved her when he'd walked out of her office yesterday and the pain of leaving her forever had outweighed the pain facing his past would cause.

He *had* simply been trading one kind of pain for another, and the pain of living without Colleen wasn't something he wanted to live with for the rest of his life.

He would gladly face his past for her. Not seeing her ever again would ultimately be more painful than dealing with his terrible memories.

A giant load lifted off his heart, and he wondered why it had taken him so long to get a clue and figure all this out. Colleen was a prize he would do anything to obtain, including publishing and dealing with more of the pictures he'd taken overseas.

Filled damn near full with anticipation, he rushed from Joe's office and headed to Colleen's cube. He rounded the corner and burst through the doorway...and she wasn't there.

He let out a heavy breath, then cast his gaze around her empty cube.

He hardly recognized the space.

It was spotlessly clean, which he hadn't noticed the last time he'd been here, every file in place, every piece of paper neatly put away. Her desk was clean and tidy, the floor was clear of bulging file folders, and two healthy plants had replaced the dead ones that had been here the day he'd first seen Colleen after he'd returned to Portland.

She'd added a few homey touches, including a photo of Laura on her desk and a few pictures of cute puppies and kittens tacked to the walls.

He dropped into the small chair in the corner, feeling shell-shocked. This wasn't the office of the disorganized, slightly flaky Colleen he'd come home to find. This was the office of an organized, in-control woman.

A woman who might not want him anymore.

He thought about that, his gaze catching on the picture of the puppy on the wall above her desk. Colleen had walked away from the puppy she'd loved so much at his parents' house, even though they were clearly meant for each other.

Just as she'd walked away from him.

A lightbulb went off in his head, and he knew exactly what he needed to do.

On Tuesday, Colleen worked all day, relishing her clean, organized office even as thoughts of Aiden haunted her. She was unable to forget his fresh, clean scent, jaw-dropping smile, and how safe and cherished she'd always felt in his arms.

She literally ached for him, but ruthlessly reminded herself that wanting him was as futile as wishing she'd turn into a unicorn. He was too caught up in his past to ever be able to love her, and even if he could, she still had too many doubts about her ability to nurture a relationship to be able to love him the way he deserved. Besides, he would never forgive her for meddling in his life.

The truth burned, but couldn't be ignored.

After work, she had dinner with her best friend, Erin, who was glowing with the news of her first pregnancy. Erin had met her husband, Jared, when she'd interviewed him for "The Bachelor Chronicles." They'd had a rocky road to finding each other, and Erin had frankly chastised Colleen for not going after Aiden.

Colleen told Erin that she just couldn't do that. She related how he'd been very clear about how angry and unforgiving he was with her for suggesting his mom turn over those pictures, and had made no secret of how unwilling he was to face his past for her.

And, really, how could she risk the pain of his probable rejection when she had so many persistent doubts about herself?

No, she had to put the fantasy of having a future with Aiden on the shelf where it had always belonged.

After work, she went home to her small house and worked on an article that was due the next day. As she worked at the pine kitchen table, doing her level best to focus on the subject of her article and not on Aiden, a pall she'd been fighting all day fell down around her, choking her with a sadness she hated. By the time she was finished editing her article, all she wanted to do was go to bed, pull the covers up over her head and sleep away her gloom.

Mercy. She was a melancholy mess.

The doorbell rang, startling her. She stood, looking at her watch: 9:30 p.m. She frowned and headed to the front door, wary. It was late.

She looked through the peephole—and saw a familiar black puppy with curly fur staring at her.

Puzzled, she drew her eyebrows together. Then the cute little puppy face was replaced with Aiden's. He cracked a wide, goofy grin.

Excitement rushed through her, lifting the dark cloud descending over her like a fresh, cleansing breeze. She sighed, wishing she wasn't so darned glad to see him.

She shoved that unfortunate information aside to focus on a more important issue.

Why was he here? And why was he smiling? The last time she saw him, he'd had steam coming out his ears.

She unlocked the door and opened it. "Aiden," she said, warily eyeing him. "What's going on? Why do you have that puppy?"

He stepped through the door as if he owned the place. "She's for you."

Colleen drew in her chin and stared at him sideways, her eyebrows hoisted high. "For me?"

"Yup." He held out the fluffball. "She's yours."

"Oh, no," she said, waving her hands in the air, backing up. "I... don't...uh, want a puppy." Oh, but she did! She wanted to take the tiny thing and hold it close and kiss it to death. But she couldn't. Now, when she was feeling so low, was not the time to be torturing herself with things she couldn't have, things that made her ache.

She'd proved how incapable she was of taking care of others by blowing it with Aiden. She still didn't have any idea how to love anybody—or anything, including a darling puppy.

"I think you do, Colleen." He held out the puppy again, a knowing smile on his face. "You held this puppy for hours at my parents'. I think you want her a lot."

She bit her lip. He was so right, and really, would it hurt to hold the baby dog for just a moment? Unable to resist the tempting little bundle of fur, she held out shaking hands and took the puppy from him.

She pulled her close and buried her nose in soft fur, breathing in puppy scent.

Her heart melted.

"Okay, then," Aiden said, moving toward the still-open door, blithely waving. "Gotta go."

Colleen looked up, widening her eyes, panic coming to life. She had no idea how to take care of a puppy. "You're leaving?" she said, rushing across the small entryway, her voice rising.

"Yeah." He gazed at her quizzically. "Is that a problem? I told you, she's yours."

She pulled a face. "Of course it is. You can't just show up on my doorstep, dump a puppy in my arms and leave. I…I can't…um, I don't know how to take care of a puppy."

He held up a finger. "I figured that." He went out to the porch and bent down. He straightened and turned, a huge basket of puppy supplies in his hands. "Here's everything you'll need, including an instruction book. She's already eaten, so you don't need to worry about that, but you will need to take her out to go potty before bedtime.''

Stunned, she sputtered, ''Oh, no, Aiden…no, no, I can't do this—''

''Sure you can.'' He patted her shoulder, his fingers burning a hole through her shirt. ''You'll figure it out.''

And then he left. Just like that, he walked away, leaving Colleen with a tiny puppy she had no idea how to take care of.

She should run after Aiden and tell—no, demand!—that he take this puppy away *right now*. But the little ball of fluff felt so warm and cozy in her arms….

Biting her lip, she looked down at the tiny thing. She was absolutely the cutest animal that Colleen had ever seen. Tentatively, following some newfound instinct that reminded her of when she'd had to take care of Laura, she snuggled her close. The puppy licked her cheek.

All over again, Colleen's heart came undone.

The feeling terrified her. Being responsible for another living thing was something she'd avoided for a long, long time. She simply didn't have it in her to take care of something else, to love and nurture it.

The puppy made a small, cute noise, clearly wanting Colleen's attention. Colleen stroked her soft, curly fur, losing herself in the feel of a tiny life in her hands. The pup looked up at Colleen, her dark eyes soft and trusting, and Colleen's chest tightened.

Even though she'd always avoided baby anythings,

she was undeniably deeply touched by Aiden's gift, overwhelmed by its sheer unexpectedness and thoughtfulness. Why, he'd actually gone to the trouble of giving her this adorable puppy! No one else had ever done something so wonderfully special for her before.

Aiden truly was a special, fantastic, one-in-a-million man.

A man she should hold on to.

Unbidden, hope skyrocketed inside her, lighting up a shadowed, dull place in her heart that had been dark forever. Was it possible that she and Aiden had a chance, that a future for them was possible? Oh, how she wished that were true—

She ruthlessly stopped that notion in its measly little tracks. Nothing had changed. She was still flawed. The puppy was just a nice gift, nothing more, and she was a fool to let her hopes soar to a forbidden place they had no business being. She needed to quit dreaming about a bright future with Aiden and focus on the here and now.

Ignoring the ache and deep sense of loss weighing her down, she held the puppy up and looked directly at her. "Okay, little one, I'll give this a go. It's just you and me." She looked down at the basketful of supplies. Holding the puppy in one hand, she bent down and dragged the basket into the adjoining living room and sat down on the small flowered couch in the corner.

She picked up the book on the top, settled the pup on her lap, opened the book and began to read.

With a darling little doggie sigh, the puppy laid her head down and closed her eyes, obviously confident all was well in her world.

Colleen wished she felt as confident.

The next morning, Colleen dragged herself out of bed, exhausted. The puppy, whom she'd christened Lexi sometime around 3:00 a.m., hadn't slept a wink for most of the night. She'd whined and cried the moment Colleen had put her in the cardboard box she'd lined with an old towel and a few worn-out, rolled-up socks.

Unable to bear Lexi's cries, Colleen had held her for part of the night, then finally fell asleep around 4:00 a.m., Lexi nestled in the crook of her arm.

Colleen still had to go to work, although she could afford to be a little late since she'd gone in early the last few mornings to catch up. She was glad for the extra time. Between pottying, feeding and general cuddling, which Colleen just couldn't resist, Lexi was one time-consuming little puppy gal.

Though Colleen felt horrible she'd have to leave Lexi for part of the day, she comforted herself with the fact that she could easily come home at lunchtime and let her out and feed her. Puppies, like human babies, ate every few hours.

Feeling good that the pup seemed no worse for wear, despite her clueless caregiver, Colleen kissed her furry head and put her in the box in the kitchen. Lexi plopped her bottom down and gazed up at her with her sad little coal-black eyes. She then lay down, put her head on her front paws and let out a tiny, pitiful don't-leave-me whine.

"Oh, you little stinker," Colleen said, unable to resist smiling. "You know exactly how to get to me, don't you?"

Lexi wagged her tail.

Colleen chewed on her lip and glanced at her watch. "All right, I'll pick you up for a few minutes, but then I have to go."

She bent down and picked Lexi up, a deep feeling of contentment moving through her, and heard the doorbell ring. With the puppy snuggled close, Colleen went through the kitchen archway to the front door and looked out the peephole.

The Great Puppy Dumper stood outside, an odd smile on his face. He waved.

A ripple of pure happiness moved through Colleen, but she tried like heck not to dwell on it. Even though Aiden would always hold a special place in her heart, she reminded herself that a future for them was absolutely impossible. She only had to think back to how she'd blown it by publishing Aiden's pictures to confirm that her flaw was still alive and kicking.

A heavy, heartbreaking weight building, she opened the door, steeling herself to resist Aiden's appeal no matter how much she wanted him.

Aiden waved again, his eyes sparkling like the ocean with the sun shining on it. "So, how's the puppy?"

She held up Lexi, again wondering about Aiden's sudden about-face. "Lexi is just fine, luckily."

He stepped inside and gently scruffed Lexi. "But she survived, didn't she?"

Colleen inclined her head and closed the door. "Of course she did." She held Lexi up and rubbed noses with her. "I took care of you, didn't I, Lexi-girl?"

"Hmm," Aiden said, moving into the living room, his face pressed into a speculative expression. "I thought you didn't know how to take care of anything."

She narrowed her eyes, the truth dawning. "Why, you sneaky man. Is that what this is all about? Showing me that I can take care of something?"

Aiden lifted one shoulder, looking all casual like. "Maybe. But you did say you don't know how to love or nurture anything, didn't you?"

She glared at him, irritated. "Yes, I did—"

"But you took care of—what did you name her? Lexi? That's perfect. Anyway, you took care of her, right?"

"That's different," she retorted, pacing the small living room, angry that he'd manipulated her like this. She stopped in front of him. "Taking care of a dog isn't the same as being able to love another person."

He reached out and stroked her cheek. "It's a matter of degree, sweetheart. I brought the puppy for two reasons. One, because you two were made for each other, and two, because I had to prove to you that you are capable of loving and taking care of something else."

Her curiosity about his change in attitude faded when he touched a blazing trail on her cheek, only to

be replaced by stark fear mixed with a heady anticipation she shouldn't be feeling. She had a sinking
idea she knew where he was going with this, and she
didn't want to set so much as a foot in that direction.
She was still afraid that the flaw her parents had buried within her would sabotage any chance she might
have with Aiden.

She turned away, hating the vulnerability welling
up, the fear of loving and failing that had paralyzed
her for as long as she could remember.

"I took care of a puppy for one night. Big deal."

He touched her shoulder and squeezed. "It is a big
deal for you." He gently pulled on her shoulder, forcing her to turn around. "I'd say you're pretty good
at all this, Colleen. I think you're just scared of love
and scared of failing. But you haven't failed, have
you?" he asked, looking deep into her eyes. "You
succeeded with Laura, you succeeded with my family,
and you succeeded with Lexi here. You've done all
the things you thought you couldn't."

His words, while so, so tempting to believe, only
made her ache inside. Her eyes burned. "How can
you say that after what I did to you?" She held back
a sob. "I thought you'd be long gone because I suggested your mom publish those pictures."

He pulled in a deep breath. "I admit I was well on
my way down that road. But something happened that
made me realize that you were right. I *do* need to face
my past in order to heal."

"What happened?" she asked, her heart thumping.
Mercy, had he listened to her after all?

"Joe asked me for more pictures."

Her stomach caved in. "Oh, Aiden, I'm sorry."

"No, don't be," he said, shaking his head. "I'm glad this happened."

"Why?" she asked, barely able to speak around the burning lump in her throat.

He looked down at her, his gorgeous green eyes homing in on her. "Because it made me realize that what you'd said was true. I was focusing on certain things hoping the *icky stuff* in my past would just go away. When Joe asked me for those pictures, I realized that something good could come from a very bad time, and that the time I spent overseas would be worth it if something positive could be done with the pictures." He smiled at her and took her shoulders in his big, warm hands. "You were right, you knew exactly what I needed—to face the dark memories in my past to make my future possible."

His future.

A future she wanted to share with him—but couldn't.

Could she?

As if reading her mind, he said, "Make something good come from what you've gone through, too, Colleen. Turn it around. End the cycle."

His words echoed in her mind, ringing so true, so right. All at once, her whole world, everything she'd always believed, was changing.

Because of Aiden.

Dear, wonderful, brave Aiden. He'd found the strength and courage to look his traumatic past in the eye and heal, to make something good come from the terrible things he'd gone through.

Could she do the same? Could she face what scared her, could she turn her bad experiences around—for him?

She felt Lexi's tiny, warm body in her arms, and she suddenly understood his motives. And, mercy upon mercy, she had to give him credit. She *had* taken care of Lexi, had instinctively known how to comfort her, and had managed Laura pretty well, too.

And she'd fit into Aiden's family, and had actually enjoyed the experience. Granted, that wasn't that big of a deal for most people, but for a woman who had never thought she had it in her to function in a family environment, it was a giant accomplishment.

Maybe she *could* do this love thing.

She looked at Aiden, a ray of hope beginning to shine. "So what are you saying?"

He took her free hand in his. "What I'm saying is this—I was too afraid that you would challenge me to examine things I didn't want to examine." He smiled, almost decimating her reluctant, foolish heart. "And you did challenge me, in so many ways. Not only did you challenge me to love by being so damn appealing, you challenged me by setting things in motion and publishing those pictures and forcing me to admit the truth."

"And what's that?" she asked, barely able to believe that so much had changed so quickly, that Aiden had taken the difficult path and grown enough to do what had to be a very, very painful thing for him.

A deep current of admiration and love raged through her. She braced herself for his answer, instinctively knowing that her future, her life, her happiness, was tied up in whatever he said.

He cupped her chin in his hand and glided his callused fingers over her cheeks. "That I *am* willing to face and deal with my past because I love you, Colleen, and I want that love to be a part of my life forever. And I think you know how to love, honey. I see it in you every day."

When he uttered the words she'd thought she'd never hear, miraculously, she wasn't scared or wary as she would have been yesterday. No, instead, something broke loose and warmth flooded her heart.

Making it wonderfully whole.

And suddenly, everything shifted and settled and she saw the truth for the first time. Aiden had shown her that she, too, had been using the excuse of her past to avoid love and the pain it had always caused her and the situations that had left their mark—her parents' desertion, being unable to make things work with Aiden eight years ago, to name a couple.

But Aiden had finally made her see that loving was something that came from deep inside, something that she did have within her, despite her loveless, painful childhood, despite what her parents had done.

He'd also shown her that what she'd gone through in the past didn't have to be her future.

Even so, letting go of everything that had protected her would be a giant leap she wasn't sure she could take. She desperately wanted to, but old habits were hard to break.

Shaking, she looked at Aiden. He was the only person on earth who could help her make the required, frightening jump. "All of this scares me," she whispered. "What if I fail? What if I can't do this right? Love is something I've never been very good at."

He pulled her close and pressed his mouth to her ear. "Let me be the judge of that. And you won't fail, because everything you need is here." He pulled away slightly and pressed a hand over her heart. "And here." He pressed her hand to his heart. "Together we can make this work. Besides," he said, his eyes full of wonderful, soul-touching love, "if you run away, think what you'll be missing." He slowly bent his head and pressed his mouth to hers.

The touch of his lips on hers, so wonderfully tender, went straight to her heart, melting away the tightly closed door guarding it like magic.

Thank heaven Aiden had shown her by so bravely facing his haunting fears that she had no choice but to do the same—for him, for love.

For them.

She pulled away and smiled up at him, prepared, *finally,* to say the words she'd never believed she would ever be able to say and be telling the absolute truth. "I love you, Aiden, with all my heart."

He gazed down at her and a huge grin appeared on his face. "Marry me, Colly. Marry me and help me start our own baby chronicle. I'd love to have a daughter who looks just like you."

Joy bubbling over inside her, she said, "Or what about a son who looks just like you?"

He kissed her nose. "How about both? As long as you're with me, I'll be happy."

And then he kissed his way across her cheek and down, settling his mouth on her lips. She kissed him back, feeling complete and whole for the first time in forever, filled with a love she'd never expected, never imagined, never dreamed would be hers.

A love that she would cherish and guard for the rest of her life.

* * * * *

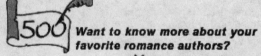

SILHOUETTE *Romance*

COMING NEXT MONTH

#1706 ONE BACHELOR TO GO—Nicole Burnham
Marrying the Boss's Daughter
Emily Winters had successfully married off all of her dad's eligible executives except one: Jack Devon, the devilishly handsome VP of Global Strategy. A business trip was her chance to learn more about the man behind the mysterious demeanor. But after sharing close quarters—and a few passionate kisses—Emily was ready to marry Jack off…
to herself!

#1707 WYATT'S READY-MADE FAMILY—
Patricia Thayer
The Texas Brotherhood
When rodeo rider Wyatt Gentry came face-to-face with sassy single mom Maura Wells, she was holding a rifle on him! The startled, sexy cowboy soon convinced her to put down the gun and give him a job on her ranch. Now if he could only convince the love-wary beauty that he was the man who could teach her and her two kids how to trust again.…

#1708 FLIRTING WITH THE BOSS—Teresa Southwick
If Wishes Were…
Everybody should have money and power, right? But despite her birthday wish, all that Ashley Gallagher got was Max Bentley, her boss's heartbreaker of a grandson. She had to convince him to stay in town long enough to save the company. And love-smitten Ashley was more than ready to use any means necessary to see that Max stayed put!

#1709 SAVED BY THE BABY—Linda Goodnight
Julianna Reynolds would do anything to save her dying daughter—even ask Sheriff Tate McIntyre to father another child! Trouble was, she'd never told him about their *first* child! Shocked, Tate would only agree to her plan if Julianna became his wife. But could their new baby be the miracle they needed to save their daughter *and* their marriage of convenience?

SRCNM0104